HAVE YOU
SEEN HER?

A Novel
Rich Silvers

CONURE PRESS

Have You Seen Her?
Rich Silvers

Printed in the United States of America.
Conure Press
145 Hitching Post Lane
Yorktown Heights, N.Y. 10598
conurepress@verizon.net

For more information about this book, visit www.richsilvers.com

Edition ISBNs
Trade Paperback 978-0-9854944-0-7
e-book 978-0-9854944-1-4

Second Edition 2013

This edition was prepared for printing by The Editorial Department
7650 E. Broadway, #308, Tucson, Arizona 85710
www.editorialdepartment.com

Cover design by Pete Garceau
Book design by Christopher Fisher

For Cathy

Acknowledgements

Thanks, Mom, for allowing me to be who I am and for introducing me to the wonder of books at a young age.

To my wife, Cathy, who supported and believed in me and became my first-read editor. Thanks, Sweetie; I couldn't have done it without you.

I knew to become a writer I needed a guide. Someone with wisdom, insight, and patience. I was blessed to find that person in Renni Browne. She was involved in the development right through the final edit, doing what great editors do, pushing me to make this story the best it can be and making me a better writer in the process.

And a big thank you to Shannon Roberts for her honesty and thoughtful suggestions that improved this manuscript along the way.

Special thanks to Ross Browne, Beth Jusino, Chris Fisher, Jane Ryder, Morgana Gallaway, Dan Grubb, Pete Garceau and the rest of The Editorial Department team. You are the best!

To Jim and Bernadette Murphy for their insights. Jim, thanks for the talks and the manuscript review you did. Your and Bernadette's contributions really made a difference.

Also, thanks to Walter Priede for his technical insights. Any mistakes are mine.

And to all my friends and family who asked about the book and supported me along the way. You all know who you are. THANK YOU.

Last but not least, thanks, Dad. I know you're up there watching, working your magic...

HAVE
YOU
SEEN
HER?

MONDAY, APRIL 2, 2007
NEW YORK CITY

HE WAS LATE. There was no getting around it. Jack Logan loathed traffic and he was stuck in a load of it.

Cars were everywhere, crowding his Mercedes, shoving their brake lights in his face. The rain came down so hard the wipers couldn't keep up.

He looked around at the drivers closest to him and saw indifference pasted on their pathetic faces. Most didn't seem to give a rat's ass that they were going nowhere fast.

"Why aren't they pissed?" Jack said as he glared at his windshield. "Something's wrong with them!"

He, on the other hand, was pissed. He, on the other hand, wanted to rip out his steering wheel, smash it through the window, and watch it bounce along the highway. No need to worry about a car running over it.

"Arguing over that stupid trade—that's what got you here," Jack said to his rearview mirror.

Humidity had seeped into his wool pants. It felt like legions of spiders were crawling up his legs.

He loosened his tie and unbuttoned his shirt collar. He checked his speedometer. All its dead needle did was remind him he still wasn't moving.

"Not even an inch."

He took deep breaths to calm himself. That didn't work. Never did. Maybe it worked for Susan, or so she claimed. None of that new-age crap ever worked for him.

Jack rammed the shift into park. He closed his eyes and visualized a crew of tow trucks up ahead grappling smashed cars. He pictured the cars around him gradually starting to move. He pictured the Mercedes starting to inch forward.

He opened his eyes. Nothing was moving. Visualization was just more new-age crap.

"Speaking of crap, that's just how you people drive!" he screamed. His throat felt raw. His fingers sped through his hair. His arm shot out, pointing at the cars in front of him. "I bet one of you talking on your cell phone caused this." He balled his hands. "Some stranger's screwing up my life." He clenched his jaw. "Dammit, Sean, why'd you pick today, huh?"

But Sean was back at their office, probably kneeling in front of his computer, praying Trident's earnings came in better than expected.

"He'd better pray."

Five years ago, Sean Sullivan had become his partner after he ponied up half a million dollars when Jack needed more capital. Now he was tired of Sean's cockiness and carelessness.

"It's getting worse."

Jack needed to confront his partner. But Jack's thing wasn't dealing with people; it was trading stocks. That he did with the best of them.

At ten-thirty this morning he and Sean had begun debating whether to keep their five thousand shares of Trident, a technology company set to announce its earnings after the market closed. The stock was volatile. Jack loved volatile stocks. He and Sean had made a lot of money off them. But Jack wanted to sell and lock in their $15K profit. Not a bad three-day return for someone who grew up poor and never went near a college.

Every so often Sean got greedy, but he knew that avoiding unnecessary risks was a key factor in Logan & Sullivan's success. Jack figured it wouldn't take much time to extract his partner's big head from his ass so he could see the light. Sean always listened to Jack…eventually.

"That's another reason I put up with him," Jack said to the bumper of the minivan ahead of him.

But Sean had been different lately. This morning his take on Trident was that the analysts had understated its revenue, which would result in a positive earnings surprise. It was a bold prediction—not unusual for Sean, but he wouldn't back down on it, which was. Jack was convinced Sean hadn't done a thorough analysis.

"He never does."

Jack had three million in his personal account, but he'd worked hard for every dime. Sean had his parents' money. Trading stocks was just something he did to keep busy—no, that wasn't fair, he loved it. But succeed or fail, Sean Sullivan was set for the rest of his life.

Stock trading was creative in its own way, but Jack wondered, not for the first time, if he shouldn't have pursued his penchant for writing as a career instead. "At least then I'd control some outcomes." He opened his window. Rain hit his face.

He'd gone through Sean's calculations and found two flaws.

First, Sean assumed Trident's new microprocessor, NEO, would outsell its predecessors by twenty percent. Based on what? His partner was seduced by the NEO buzz. Jack became skeptical when too many people were optimistic on paper.

Second, Sean underestimated how much NEO would eat into the sales of Trident's existing product line.

Sean listened to Jack's careful, logical explanations but insisted that NEO's potential trumped both points.

That's when Jack's assistant, Marjorie Nichols, interrupted them to tell Jack that Susan was on the line. Jack checked his watch and his stomach hit the floor. It was eleven-thirty. He and Sean had been going at it for an hour. He should be halfway home by now.

"Tell her I just left, will you? I'm out the door now."

Jack and Susan had been married for two years. He was forty-two. She was thirty-five and looked twenty-five. She was also six months pregnant with a girl they'd already named Alison.

This morning Susan had held him tight and whispered she was bleeding. It hit him like a swift kick in the gut. Susan called the obstetrician as soon as the office opened. She was as nervous as she was beautiful, and Dr. Gunn wanting to see her that afternoon did nothing to calm her.

"I should've called Gunn myself."

Jack had insisted they go to Dr. Neil Gunn even though his office was in the city. Gunn was rated the best obstetrician in the state.

Susan wasn't impressed, but Jack hired the best and the birth of their daughter was no time to make an exception.

Susan had a phobia about driving in the city and agreed to go to Gunn only after Jack promised he'd take her to every appointment. It hadn't seemed like a problem then.

Jack's office was an hour from home and it was another hour to the doctor from there. That was with normal traffic. He'd planned to leave his office at eleven, figuring even with traffic he'd be on time. He loved his wife and couldn't wait to be a father, but somehow work had taken precedence over his marriage—again.

Susan tolerated his self-centeredness. He was sure she'd

never leave him. But if he didn't change, she'd stop loving him—a fate worse than divorce.

His cell phone rang. He grabbed it and pressed the talk button.

"How's it going?" Marjorie asked. Besides Susan, Marjorie was the only person he trusted.

"I'd rather be having a root canal," Jack said, dazed by the metronome movement of his windshield wipers. "In fact, make it a double."

"Good you haven't lost your sense of humor."

"I feel like I'm losing my mind." Jack took his foot off the brake. The car was in park. "I'm stuck. There's a three-car accident up ahead."

"Should I call Susan and tell her you'll be late?"

"Thanks, but even Susan would have a problem with that. I need to call her myself."

The rain slowed. Now it was only pouring. A young woman in a business suit stood outside her car under an umbrella, craning her neck. A gust of wind snuck up behind her and blew the umbrella out of her hand. Was she having a worse day than him?

"Is there anything I can do?" Marjorie asked.

"Get me a helicopter."

"Jack," Marjorie said. He imagined her smiling, shaking her head.

"You have any idea what's up with Sean?" Jack watched the woman chase her umbrella, getting drenched. "I know he likes to come up with his own ideas, but he's taking assertiveness to a whole new level."

"Must be those seminars he's attending. One's called 'Taking Back Control of Your Life.' Call Susan. Talk to you later."

The dashboard clock read 12:10.

He was fifty minutes from home without traffic. No way he'd get there on time. He dialed his home number.

"Please tell me you're almost here," Susan said after the first ring.

"I'm near the expressway." His long fingers combed his dark curly hair. "But nobody's moving. There's an accident."

"What time did you leave?"

"Eleven-forty." Jack crossed fingers. "But even if I'd left—"

"You still wouldn't have made it." There was real pain in her voice. "How could you do this to me?"

He looked out the passenger window. The kid in the Honda next to him was playing his dashboard like a piano.

Susan let out a breath. "I'm going by myself."

"You can't."

"Gunn has surgery this afternoon. He's leaving at two." He thought he'd lost the connection until she said, "You've left me no choice."

Click.

That's how Susan handled things. She didn't yell and rarely cursed. Sometimes he wished she would—an occasional screaming match might do them good.

The minivan in front of him started moving. He was about to call Susan and tell her to wait when it came to an abrupt halt. He stomped on the brake to avoid hitting its bumper.

He shut his eyes. The back of his eyelids burned. He pictured Susan staring out the living room window, collecting herself before she made the drive he promised her she'd never have to make. He could smell the clean scent of her hair. He could feel the beauty mark on the side of her lip—the one he traced with his finger after they made love. He saw anger in her clear blue eyes. Still, he was sure she'd forgive him for letting her down. That almost made it worse.

Jack slipped back to the moment when Susan first told him about her fear of driving in the city. It was just an aspect of her then, like her not eating red meat. At the time he couldn't imagine it ever being a complication.

It was the morning after their first night together. They were in Susan's bed—under a white down comforter. March sunshine spilled into the room.

"Tell me what you fear most." Susan liked asking questions.

He leaned over and gently kissed her lips. He had wanted to say "losing you," but those words got stuck in his throat. Was telling someone what he feared most what he feared most?

"Driving in the city scares the hell out of me," Susan said.

"That's your worst fear?" He stroked her hair.

"It's big to me." She moved away from him and studied the ceiling.

"Come on, Susan." He smiled. "You don't have any real problems."

"Screw you, Jack." The first and last time he'd heard her curse. "Just because I don't wear my problems like a badge of honor doesn't mean I don't have any."

"And I do?"

"Sometimes you act as if being unhappy is the only intelligent way to live. I don't like that about you."

"Tell me about your fear," he said after seconds of silence that felt like minutes. He hoped the sincerity in his heart made it to his voice.

He couldn't lose her.

She took a deep breath. She wasn't staring at the ceiling anymore, but past it.

"The tall buildings…I feel like they're about to fall," she said. "It's like I'm suffocating, then I'm afraid I'll black out."

Their bodies weren't touching, but he still felt the tremor from hers as she described her fear. Had making love left a temporary connection between them or was it something more enduring than that?

"How'd you find out you had this phobia?" He was better at asking questions than answering them.

"The hard way." She smiled.

"Tell me."

She ran her finger along the comforter. "A year after graduation I had to drive to the city to meet a friend from college. I'd never driven there before and was anxious about it, but I convinced myself I just needed to get on the road and I'd be fine." Her hands turned into fists. "I was—until I got into the middle of the city with those damn skyscrapers. I couldn't breathe. That's the last thing I remember before I drove through a storefront window." She winced. "Luckily, I didn't hit the elderly woman standing next to it."

"Did you get hurt?" He felt a chill.

"They said the airbag saved my life. The car was totaled and my insurance company paid the fifty-thousand for property damage. So you see, Mr. Logan, bad things can and do happen to me."

He stroked her cheek with the back of his hand.

"I'll never drive down there again." She fell back on the pillow and crossed her arms.

And she wouldn't be if—

A horn honked.

Jack opened his eyes.

The minivan was half a car length away.

He checked his rearview mirror.

Through raindrops he saw the driver of the SUV behind him move his lips and slap his steering wheel. The driver looked Jack's age. He had short dark hair and a manicured beard. Jack had the habit of naming strangers. He named this one Zeke.

Jack tapped the accelerator until he was inches from the minivan's bumper. He looked in his rearview mirror.

"Are we happy now, Zeke?" Jack shook his head. "I should've named you Dick."

Jack turned the radio on to the business station. He pictured Sean at his computer, high on adrenaline, waiting for Trident's earnings.

Jack wished he was back there with him. He wanted to hide in the shell of what he was good at. He thought marriage and the impending birth of his daughter would transform him into who he wanted to be, or at least into someone who could get his priorities straight.

He still had a lot further to go.

CHAPTER 1

SUSAN LOGAN ALWAYS WORE WHITE. On most days, it was the only color she wore. All the rooms in her house were painted white. Most of her furniture was white. So were her towels and linens. And during her daily meditation, she imagined she was floating inside a ball of white light, one that kept her safe from harm.

After Susan hung up on Jack, she stood by their loveseat and looked out the picture window behind it. It was raining. Hard. She'd be driving in Manhattan in a deluge because Jack had put his work first—again.

"It's more than just work," she said. "It's time you faced that." Like her husband, Susan never let the absence of a listener stop her when she wanted to speak her mind.

She put her hand on her belly and felt a kick. She prayed the solution to her Jack problem was growing inside her.

She padded toward the bedroom. She felt like a fat waddling duck even though everyone said her pregnancy hardly showed.

She passed the picture of her parents on the dresser—her father's arm wrapped around her mother as she leaned into him. "Thirty-seven years and I still tingle when he touches me," her mother said. Susan once believed she'd have that with Jack. Now, after just two years, she wasn't sure.

She stepped out of her slippers and into her favorite sneakers. They were a year old but still as white as on the day she bought them. Too bad everything in life wasn't like that. She bent down and tied the laces tight—but not too tight.

She froze.

Balance, that's what was missing from their relationship. Jack was going to be a father. He didn't have the luxury of time to make the changes he needed to make. Couldn't he see that?

She wanted to call him and unleash the anger locked inside her while he stewed in traffic. It would feel so good to let it out.

"Once and for all!"

But Jack had only met her true anger once, after their first night together. His saying she didn't have any problems had hit a nerve he didn't know existed.

Susan stepped in front of her dresser and ran a brush through her hair. Opposite the picture of her parents was one of her and Jack taken on their first New Year's Eve together. Things were still good then. The few who had met both Jack and Susan's ex-boyfriend, Alan, thought they looked a lot alike—black hair, deep-set blue eyes, tall, thin.

Alan Dean, professor of English at Whitmore College, was the first man Susan had ever loved. She thought he'd be the last. But then he fell in love with another student—a skinny girl who always wore black clothes and too much mascara.

Susan figured Alan would come back to her. He married the skinny girl instead.

After Susan met Jack, she was grateful it hadn't worked out between her and Alan, but now most of that feeling was gone.

She slid open the door to her closet and started searching for her favorite white blouse—the one she'd bought while at a seminar on personal power. The blouse would give her the strength to do what she swore she'd never attempt. Fortunately, she'd anticipated this day and prepared for it. She visualized making that dreaded drive before she got out of bed most mornings.

Alison kicked again.

Better find that blouse.

Which wasn't in the closet. She knelt by the white wicker laundry chest in front of their brass bed. She opened it slowly, as if this would improve her odds of finding what she needed.

She pulled clothes from the chest, flinging them over her shoulders, moving faster, like a crazed game show contestant.

"Come on, Susan, a little more and you win that trip to Mexico!"

She found the blouse at the bottom of the chest.

Sitting back on her heels, she stretched out the blouse's arms and sniffed various parts of it.

"Eeeeeuw." The blouse had been next to Jack's crew socks, now curled up by her knee. "Even when he's not here he's an obstacle."

Susan looked at the digital clock on the oak nightstand. Her stomach knotted as she stuffed the dirty laundry back into the chest. She put the blouse in last, giving herself one final chance to decide if she could wear it despite the odor. But when she discovered Jack's smelly socks were still by her knee, she threw them at the blouse and slammed the lid. She blew a wisp of hair away from her face, pushed off the floor, and went back to her closet. She'd let fate take charge and wear the first blouse her hands found. That sometimes worked.

Panic seized her when she pulled out a black blouse—a gift from Jack she wore just often enough so he wouldn't know she hated it. She considered making another try but knew she really didn't have time for decisions.

She took off her white smock and flung it on the bed. Buttoned the black blouse while she headed for the kitchen.

She grabbed her white pocketbook off the center island and a cream windbreaker from a thick dinette chair. She went into the garage, pushed a button, and the door made a quiet ascent. Jack had looked for weeks for a silent garage door opener. "Listen," he said after the men who installed it left. "You hardly hear it." Susan wished he put that kind of focus on their marriage.

She avoided a poke from a bicycle's handlebars as she slithered to the back of her white Lexus to make sure no children were there. It was raining, and the little rugrats should be inside, but she always erred on the side of caution and had yet to regret it.

After confirming all was clear, she slid into her car and breathed in its rich leather scent, still there after two years. The Lexus had been a surprise wedding present from Jack. He'd parked it in the driveway with a giant bow on its roof. When he uncovered her eyes to show it to her, she had the same thought she had now—a car was something a husband and wife should buy together, even when it was a present. That's how her parents were.

She turned the ignition key. The dashboard glowed soft white light. Raindrops pelted the windshield after she backed out of the garage. She turned on her wipers. She'd always visualized making this drive on a sunny day. The rain made everything—

Don't go there.

Ten minutes later, Susan was in the right lane on the parkway. It had two lanes and a speed limit of forty-five. She wished she could stay on it for the entire trip. But no, her husband had seen to that. Her body shook. She focused on breathing.

A late-model sedan pulled in front of her. It was white and moved at a steady pace.

"I'm following you."

She passed the exit for the obstetrician her sister, Emily, had suggested. Her hands tightened on the wheel.

"Gunn's the best," Jack had held up the magazine article that said so. "How could you want anything less for our baby?" Jack used guilt when he wanted his way. It had worked in the past.

"But it never will again."

A month after her first appointment with Gunn, she and Emily were having lunch at Daniela's and Emily's obstetrician friend walked in.

Melanie Steers wore a white pantsuit and a warm smile. After talking with her for five minutes, Susan felt as if she'd known the tall, slender woman her entire life.

"She should be delivering my baby." Susan felt a pang of regret. "Not some celebrity doctor who's always in a rush." She turned on the stereo and was surrounded by an angelic voice. She imagined the road in front of her was a beam of white light that would lead her safely to her destination.

Time passed. She felt peaceful.

The white sedan exited.

Susan looked up and saw the amber metal bridge.

The bridge looked rusty. It looked like any minute one of its bolts would give way and it would collapse into the dirty water below. Susan shivered. She had to take that bridge while crossing over two lanes to get onto the East River Drive.

She adjusted her hands on the wheel, like a batter waiting for a pitch. She punched off the stereo as her tires moaned over the bridge's grooved metal pavement. Her heart beat faster.

Over her right shoulder she saw a black van and a convertible parallel with her in the two lanes she had to cross. In her rearview mirror she saw a ten-wheeler. She put on her right blinker and eased off the accelerator, doing her best to let the truck's driver know she was trying to get behind the van on her right.

The truck's horn blared as it moved closer.

She bit her lower lip.

The vehicle in front of her sped up.

She sucked in a breath, gave the Lexus more gas, and turned the wheel.

She closed her eyes.

When she opened them, she was one lane over and the van was behind her.

Two heartbeats later she slipped in front of the convertible, then onto the exit for the Drive. It wasn't the smoothest maneuver, but she just made it without knocking over any of the yellow barrels bundled on her left.

She banked the curve of the exit ramp and freed the breath trapped inside her since who knew when. She checked her rearview mirror. The van was behind her. She wished it wasn't black.

She got onto the Drive and stayed in the right lane. The van followed her. She kept below the speed limit. "Get out of my life!" she said to the rearview mirror.

Moments later, the van zipped past her. It weaved around vehicles then vanished.

Her muscles relaxed just a bit.

A green sign said the First Avenue exit was one mile ahead. She sat up straight and held the wheel at four and eight. It was the last leg of the journey. The one that terrified her the most.

Her eyes widened.

That damn black van was stalled in her lane. She slowed to get over before she reached it, but no one let her in.

"You're all bastards."

She slammed on the brakes, her chest churning with anger while cars flew by the Lexus. She imagined them bursting into oblivion, skeet shooting them in her mind.

The center lane opened up. She stepped on the gas, whipped around the stalled van, and darted for the exit. A stop light was at the end of it. The rain came down harder. Skyscrapers were lined up on either side of her.

She went back to that day a dozen years ago—the day her fear was born. She could still feel the jolt of her car hitting that building and hear the sound of metal crumpling—screeching as if it were in pain.

She took deep breaths. They didn't calm her.

The light was still red.

She opened her pocketbook and pulled out the sonogram of Alison. Her fingers grazed the black and white image.

"It's just me and you."

The light turned green. She put the picture on the passenger seat. Her hands found the wheel, her foot pressed the accelerator, and her car knifed through the intersection.

She kept driving.

As she made her way down the next block, a car pulled out of a parking space. She swerved around it. Her car hit a pothole. It landed with a thud and gave her a jolt.

She blinked. Everything was clearer.

She looked up. The tall buildings weren't going to fall on her. She could breathe.

She felt lighter with each block she put behind her. She'd get to the doctor on time and he'd tell her everything was fine. Now she was looking forward to seeing Jack's doctor. Imagine that.

Susan was three blocks from Gunn's office. She opened her windows even though it was still raining. She didn't care—she wanted fresh air. She felt free!

She imagined her anger towards Jack floating up to the sky, evaporating.

"We can fix our marriage," she said.

Jack hadn't been there for her and he'd helped her because he wasn't.

"Thank you, Jack."

She smiled. It had worked out for the best, after all. She

laughed. Laughed so hard tears were in her eyes. She didn't care if someone saw her and thought she was crazy. It was time to celebrate. She had conquered her fear!

The light ahead of her turned green. She drove faster.

A truck was double-parked at the corner she was heading toward. A man was unloading boxes, bringing them into Way-Lo Electronics. Why not make Jack buy her a TV for their exercise room—a big one. And you know what? They'd buy it from Way-Lo Electronics.

"Now that's apropos."

They'd go together and *she'd* drive. She pictured Jack in the passenger seat, watching her, amazed, proud as they talked about what they'd do to get their relationship back to where it once was.

She could call and tell him what she wanted as soon as she parked. It would only take a minute. She had time. She'd make him grovel a little just for the fun of it, then tell him how she had overcome her fear and how this had given her the courage to face and fix what was wrong with their marriage. She'd own up to letting the status quo go on longer than it should have instead of just telling him what her needs were. She smiled, knowing she could do this, knowing Jack would work with her.

On the same side of the street, right before the electronics store, was a topless bar. Ugh. Awful places that degraded the women who worked there, took advantage of their low self-esteem. She'd like to—

A young woman with blond hair in a short white dress was about to enter the bar. A horn honked. The girl stopped, turned, and looked at Susan.

Susan knew those eyes, that mouth. It felt like her insides were being ripped from her.

"Why are you going in there?" she asked. Then she screamed her baby's name.

The young woman looked confused.

There was no place to pull over.

Red and orange police lights were in Susan's rearview mirror. She heard a siren. She heard a voice through a bullhorn: "Keep moving."

"Dammit!"

Her heart pounded, perspiration soaked her. She turned around—she couldn't lose the young woman.

Their eyes found each other's again.

But the young woman was pointing, her mouth moving frantically, terror etched on her face.

"What's she saying?"

Oh. The Lexus was still moving forward. Too late, she remembered the truck double-parked at the end of the block and slammed on the brakes.

CHAPTER 2

HIS LIFE WAS CLEANLY CUT IN HALF. The things he did before the accident. The things he did after.

After the accident, Jack Logan felt dirty. He always felt dirty. He washed his hands constantly. He showered and changed his clothes twice a day. He still felt dirty. Everything he touched felt dirty.

He vacuumed, dusted, and cleaned everywhere, including behind the refrigerator.

It's always a bitch moving that.

He scrubbed his bathrooms on his knees until bleach burned his eyes and his fingers bled. It barely helped.

Everything still feels so dirty.

Jack opened his mail as soon as it came and paid every bill immediately. Afterwards he couldn't leave outgoing mail in his house or even in the mailbox. He had to bring it to the post office or he'd go out of his mind.

He'd never liked clutter. Now he hated it, hated it with a passion that burned white hot inside him, turning him into a stranger.

His obsessions grew like weeds, wrapping their roots around his brain, dictating his every move. He prayed to a higher power he couldn't find the faith to believe in, begging for mercy.

You need to make me stop. I need a break. Even for an afternoon. Please.

His prayers went unanswered, and he knew why—he didn't deserve mercy. Not one bit.

Every morning he made sure every drawer was in perfect order. If a drawer got stuck he'd want to yank it out and smash it to bits, but he couldn't destroy anything. He'd destroyed too much already.

All he could do was correct the problem. He had to correct every problem he found immediately, and he couldn't stop finding them.

Jack worked methodically and maniacally from morning till night, removing clutter and cleaning everything he could, everywhere he could. He had to discard at least ten items each day, but none that had belonged to Susan. Those, he couldn't even touch.

Your hands are too dirty for that.

He allowed himself one junk drawer, the lone exception to his now immaculate life. He could put anything in that drawer. Any way he wanted.

It just can't get stuck.

His junk drawer was a small drawer. He used it sparingly, as if he were rationing the last of his food. It was his last hold on reality. Or the way back to the man he once was, assuming he ever found a reason to be that man again.

Jack was driving home from the supermarket with two gallons of bleach, three bottles of hand sanitizer, and five cans of soup he'd throw out to meet his daily discard quota. But when he stopped for a light, he realized he couldn't throw the soup away—he hated waste as much as he hated clutter.

There's no escape.

A horn blew. He looked up. The light was green. But he kept his foot on the brake and buried his face in his hands. The car in back of him squealed around him.

Jack imagined his obsessions eating his sanity like rats gnawing a piece of cheese.

Soon there'll be nothing left.

At least he knew the cause of his illness, the exact moment it began.

It was the last time his cell phone rang, playing the first few notes of Mozart's *A Little Night Music.* Dum, da *dum,* da dum da dum dee *dum!*

"Mr. Logan?"

"Yes."

Would Susan still be alive if he'd said no, it wasn't him?

"Your wife's been in a car accident."

"How badly is she hurt?"

"I'm sorry, Mr. Logan."

Jack couldn't speak. Or breathe.

"Mr. Logan?"

They deemed it driver error. But he knew whose fault it was that his wife and unborn daughter were dead.

Jack's dashboard clock read 2:10 p.m. when he turned onto his block and saw the mail truck two houses past his. He pressed his remote and the garage door opened. He drove in, got out, and walked down the driveway to his mailbox.

Inside was a postcard. The sun hit his eyes just as his ever-friendly neighbor Fred waved to him. Jack placed the postcard between the two gallon jugs of bleach in his shopping bag, waved at Fred, and went back up his driveway.

Once inside his house he removed his outdoor shoes and stepped into his inside pair. He put the jugs of bleach under the sink. He stacked the cans of chicken soup in the pantry. Maybe he'd eat the stuff after all. Maybe it would be good for his soul.

He folded the shopping bag where it had been creased, went into the garage, and placed it in the recycle bin. He turned to leave, then realized the postcard was still in the bag. Had to be junk mail, but he couldn't ignore it. His mind wouldn't let him.

He stuck his hand inside the bag and pulled the postcard out expecting to see an advertisement for a rug cleaning service or a plumber who'd do any job no matter the size.

The postcard was blank.

Huh?

He turned the card over. On the other side was a picture of a young girl with blond hair and questioning eyes.

He looked at it. He didn't believe it. He studied it. His hands shook.

Seconds became minutes.

Now his legs were trembling.

The girl resembled Susan—no, she looked almost *exactly* like Susan.

And she was missing. Above the black and white image were four words: Have You Seen Her?

He closed his eyes. His mind raced.

Time passed.

He scaled the stairs two at a time. He went into the spare bedroom. He slept there now. A heavy-duty shredder sat in the corner, next to his dresser. He placed the postcard near the shredder's silver mouth.

He hesitated. Maybe he should keep it.

He pushed the postcard closer.

The shredder came to life, its teeth grinding, devouring what he fed it. Then it screeched to a halt.

CHAPTER 3

TWO DAYS LATER JACK was in his living room when he heard a vehicle stop and start up again after a couple of minutes. If it was the mail truck it would stop…now. It did. As soon as it drove past his block, he went out the front door into another warm, sunny day. He wished it were cloudy.

He walked quickly down his driveway, relieved not to see Fred or any of his other neighbors. He grabbed his mail and headed back up his driveway. Had he gotten it all?

He stopped, turned around, and checked his mailbox again. Before the accident he never knew doubt. Now it was his constant companion.

Back in his house, he stood in the hallway and went through the mail. He had to process this fresh batch of clutter.

They deliver it right to your mailbox, how convenient.

On top, a legal-sized envelope trumpeted a no-fee credit card. *You shred that.*

A Talbot's catalogue had a young woman on its cover wearing sandals, a stylish sunhat, and a casual yellow two-piece outfit. Jack's eyes went straight to the mailing label: Ms. Susan Logan.

Just a mailing label, and WHAM! It was a warm Sunday afternoon in October and he was on the sun porch with Susan—barefoot, wearing a loose, white cotton sundress, one leg thrown over the arm of a white wicker loveseat. Her blond hair hid her face as she flipped through a catalogue, dog-earing some pages when her eyes lit up. She had the bluest eyes.

He sat across from her on a matching chair, the sun that spilled into the room creating a circle of light between them. He was finishing a crime novel, about to find out if the psychiatrist was the serial killer.

"What do you think of this?" Susan held the catalogue against her chest.

"Too short," Jack said as he closed the book.

"Surprised to hear you say that." A smile broke on her face. She turned a page. "Then how about this?" She stretched out on the loveseat like a cat waking from a nap.

"Too long?" He grinned and slid the book onto an end table.

"Hmmm..." Susan purred. "I know what you're going to say about *this* one."

"Too white; you have too many white clothes already."

"I can never have too many white clothes." She put her heels on the arm of the loveseat. The hem of her dress fell back, exposing more thigh.

He wanted to carry her into the bedroom.

"What about this?" Her dress strap fell off her shoulder.

"Too revealing."

"That's another surprise."

"I'm full of them."

She laughed. "You're full of something."

"Of love for you," he said.

"This is conservative, what do you think?" She held the catalogue in front of her face.

"Not sexy enough."

"I'll give you sexy." Her bare feet thumped against the wood floor. She tossed the catalogue onto the loveseat and stood above him. She pulled her dress over her head.

Alison was conceived that afternoon.

Jack took a deep breath and moved the Talbot's catalogue to the bottom of the pile. His electric bill was on top of a health food supermarket flyer with color pictures of organic fruits and vegetables. His stomach growled, but his hunger would have to wait. He had to pay his electric bill and deliver it to the post office first.

He headed to the recycle bin.

Waste and bill payments: two things that never end.

As he walked through the kitchen, a postcard slipped out of the flyer and floated down to the white marble floor.

The side of the card that faced him was blank.

The hand that picked it up trembled. He turned it over.

It was the same girl.

The same words were over the photo: Have You Seen Her?

The missing girl had Susan's nose, Susan's wide eyes and high cheekbones. It wasn't a likeness. She could be Susan's twin.

How is that possible?

A chill ran down his spine.

Her name was Alyson Walker. Alyson spelled with a Y where his had an I.

They're the same but different.

The postcard said Alyson was last seen six months ago, in Ridgewood—not far from his house.

Jack placed the postcard on the center island and stared at it, not moving, not thinking—

The telephone rang.

It was 2:02 p.m. The LCD on the handset read Private Caller. He considered not answering, but his hand picked up on the third ring.

"Jack?" A woman's voice, deeper than Susan's.

You don't want to talk to her.

Jack pressed his lips together.

"Hello?"

"Hello, Emily." He hadn't been comfortable with Susan's half-sister before the accident. They hadn't spoken since the funeral.

"How are you doing?" She sounded sincere.

"You're polite to ask."

"Polite? Jack, this is Emily, remember?"

"Can I take a rain check on answering?"

"Susan was right. You don't like questions."

"It's one of my lesser flaws." He shifted the phone to his other hand. His throat was dry. He suppressed an urge to sneeze.

"I need a favor." Emily pulled in a breath, no doubt a drag on a cigarette.

He felt trapped.

"I'm listening." He shoved his hand deep into his pocket. His fingernail dug into its seam.

"You free for lunch Tuesday?" She exhaled.

He imagined smoke rolling out of her mouth. He inhaled, could smell the smoke, felt it choking him. He couldn't have lunch with Emily, sit in a restaurant and pretend his life wasn't unraveling. He just couldn't.

"Where and when?" He wiped his forehead. He'd do this for Susan. She'd want him to, wouldn't she?

"Daniela's at one?" Emily asked.

"What's this about?"

"I need help, Jack."

It wasn't like Emily to ask for help—one of the many things they had in common.

"You still there?" she asked.

The doorbell rang.

Never thought you'd be glad to hear that sound.

"Emily, someone's at the door. I'll see you Tuesday."

"Don't be late."

He heard a click and stared at the handset. He wondered if Emily had quite meant to say that.

The bell rang again. Jack slammed the phone in its cradle and went to open the door.

"Hi."

"Hi yourself." In a sleeveless blue shirt, tennis shorts, and sneakers, Marjorie looked a lot younger than her fifty-two years.

"I just got off the phone with Emily." He didn't know what else to say. Conversation had never been a problem with them in the past. The day he interviewed her they talked for two hours, mostly *after* he offered her the job. That was twelve years ago. He'd never regretted it.

Marjorie was giving him a fishy look.

"What?" he said. His mouth tasted like copper. His body ached. He slipped his hands in his pockets again. Now there was a hole in one of them.

"Jack, you look like shit."

"That's what you came to tell me?" The electric bill needed to be paid. He twitched.

You need to get rid of her. NOW!

Marjorie shook her head.

He tucked in his dress shirt and pushed back his hair. His pants hung low on his waist. He'd lost seventeen pounds since the accident. He wanted to pull his belt in another notch, maybe two, but not in front of Marjorie. At least he showered this morning. He still felt dirty, though. And he probably smelled, too.

"Emily called to see how you're doing?" Marjorie knew they weren't close. She was trying to see over Jack's shoulder.

"She wants to have lunch with me." Jack leaned on the door jamb, blocking Marjorie's view. "She says I'm the only one who can help her."

Why the hell are you prolonging this conversation?

"How do you feel about that?" Marjorie seemed to be measuring his words, gestures, probably using them to help her figure out what she needed to do.

That's Marjorie.

"I don't know." All he knew was that he needed to pay that bill and she needed to leave.

Before he could even think how to get rid of her, she was around him and inside the house. He turned and got one of her patented What-are-you-*thinking?* looks.

You're defenseless against those.

"You do a lousy self-pity." She stood in the hallway, sniffing. "Bleach?"

"I've been doing some cleaning." Jack felt his face turn red.

"I'll say. This place is immaculate." She shrugged. "Come on, I'll make you something to eat."

"I'm not hungry." His stomach growled. His checkbook was up in his bedroom. He needed to get it.

"Jack, look at you. Your pants are falling down. Your face is gaunt. I'd say you haven't had a decent meal in weeks."

He'd been living on frozen macaroni and cheese. He'd have to try another brand.

"Marjorie, this is a bad time. I have some things to take care of."

"Don't worry, I can't stay long." She moved toward the kitchen, surveying her surroundings like a Marine on patrol.

"I'll be right back." He shot up the stairs.

Shit, Alyson's postcard is on the center island.

He barged into his bedroom, grabbed his checkbook, and ran back down the stairs. Slipped on the last step and landed hard on his tailbone. He bit his finger, stifling his scream. He didn't move.

Silence. No call from Marjorie asking if he was all right. He'd once broken a toe on his way to the bathroom in the middle of the night. Susan woke when he cried out and held him. Now he sucked in a breath and got up slowly. The checkbook lay open, face down like an innocent victim.

He picked it up and limped down the hall, fearing he'd find Marjorie studying Alyson's postcard. Instead she was studying the contents of his refrigerator. She straightened up and faced him.

"I could make an omelet, a grilled cheese. . . .What do you want?"

"To be left alone." His tailbone throbbed. He wanted to scream.

"Cut the Garbo crap, Jack. You *have* been left alone, and it hasn't done you a damn bit of good." She let the refrigerator door close and stood in front of him. Her breath was minty. "I'm worried about you," she said.

He dropped the checkbook on top of Alyson's postcard. "I'm doing the best I can." He turned his back to Marjorie and slid the postcard behind the last check. He took it and the electric bill over to the dinette table. Marjorie followed him.

"You're limping."

"That's because I broke my ass." He sat slowly and felt a sharp pain like a stiletto piercing him from within.

Marjorie watched him.

He ripped the electric bill at the perforation. The tear wasn't clean. *Damn.* He got scissors and cut it. His heart was racing. He checked the clock above the sink: nearly three. The post office was across town. It closed at four.

Not much time if traffic is bad.

"What are you doing?"

"I'm paying the electric bill." Jack wrote out the check, felt calmer.

"Can't it wait?" She put her hands on her hips.

He looked up. "The post office closes in an hour."

"Scheduling your payments so tight? Are you in financial trouble?"

"Money isn't the problem." He put the check and the payment stub in the envelope. The envelope moistener was up in his bedroom. He closed his eyes, licked the glue, and sealed it.

Shit, is the address showing?

He turned the envelope over. It was.

He held the envelope up to the light but couldn't see through it.

"You wrote the account number on the check," Marjorie said. He felt naked. He crossed his legs. "You haven't been to work in three months. When are you coming back?"

"I have no desire to trade. That's a perfect way to lose money." He'd slice open the envelope after Marjorie left. He still had to check the account number.

"Bull. And don't give me any of that crap about Sean not needing you. We both know he's going to fall sooner or later, and you'd better be there to catch him when he does. Besides, it'll be good for you to get back to what you're good at."

"Has fixing my life been added to your job description?"

"You were never self-destructive, Jack. Don't start now."

Two weeks after the accident Marjorie had called and asked if she could come over. It was a dark, rainy day, too much like the one Susan died on. Marjorie brought sandwiches and they ate at the kitchen table, mostly in silence. That time she just let him be.

You knew she wouldn't do that for long.

"Give it a few days and see how it goes," Marjorie said. "You can always go back to whatever it is you've been doing."

"I'll think about it." He didn't have to, but even without his money he was done trading. He was sure of that.

"You'll think about it?" Marjorie shook her head. "You've got to do better than that."

"I can't see myself ever coming back." He stood up.

"What are you going to do?" Marjorie was in front of him. Her hands found his arms. He flinched. She let go as if she'd been burned. "You sit around this house all day and you'll go out of your mind."

Too late.

"Marjorie, when I'm ready to talk you'll be the first one I call." He wasn't lying, he just didn't know when that would be.

She looked at her watch. She probably had to leave.

He moved out of her reach.

"Talk to me." Her eyes pleaded.

GO AWAY! The words exploded in his head even as he yearned to confide.

A minute passed. Two? More?

"Okay, Jack. You win."

Does this look like winning?

She turned and walked away. He doubled over.

She's the last person left who cares about you.

He cradled himself as he heard the front door close.

CHAPTER 4

JACK OPENED HIS REFRIGERATOR. Inside were foods and liquids in plastic, cardboard, and metal containers. How many similar containers were in all the other refrigerators on his block, waiting to be discarded?

Waste. It's everywhere.

He snatched a quart of milk from the top shelf. He held the refrigerator door handle as cool air hit his face, only to slam it shut with the thought that he was wasting electricity.

If you're not part of the solution, you're part of the problem. It's as simple as that.

He got a tall glass and went to the kitchen table with its thick glass top and six white leather swivel chairs gathered around it as if for a meeting. He poured the milk slowly, watched it turn the glass a rich shade of white. A children's chorus sang inside his head.

The ceilings are white. The walls are white. Every room in this house is white!

The furniture is white. Fridge and stove are white. Everything in sight is white!

"WHITE IS ALL OVER THE PLACE!"

Jack took sharp, short breaths as if he were hyperventilating. He was on the ledge of sanity, toes hanging over it, heels coming off it. He looked down into an abyss.

Jump.

He gulped the milk down, nearly all of it.

It soothed his throat, raw from bleach fumes. When he put the glass down he saw the tips of his fingers.

Shit, they do look burnt.

The clock above the white stove said 10:05. Today was Monday. He'd meet Emily for lunch in less than twenty-seven hours. Maybe she'd call and cancel.

You should be so lucky.

The phone rang.

Jack gave a start.

Could it be Emily?

Caller ID said it was his office. Two more rings. He went to the hallway and stood with one hand on the banister at the foot of the stairs. The answering machine was up in his bedroom.

"Jack." It was Sean. "Are you there? Please pick up if you are.... I was just wondering how you're doing."

Jack hadn't spoken to his partner since Susan's funeral.

"Okay...well, please give me a call when you can.... Take care."

Jack went back into the kitchen. He smelled something rancid.

Hold on, you just cleaned.

He sniffed. Caught a faint whiff of something that smelled like rotting garbage.

On the refrigerator he kept two lists—one for things to do, the other for things to buy. He wrote *clean kitchen* on the first list and *milk* on the second.

Before last week, he hadn't drunk milk since he was a teenager. Then he had it with cereal and enough sugar so he got some on every spoonful.

He picked up the empty milk carton and read its nutritional label. When he turned the container around and saw Alyson Walker on the other side, it felt like a hand had reached into his chest and grabbed his heart.

He shut his eyes.

He opened them. The picture was still there.

Above it was the same question: Have You Seen Her? The photo was grainy, nowhere near as clear as the one on the postcard. But that didn't stop Alyson Walker from looking exactly like his wife.

How can that be?

He let go of the container and it fell on top of the table. Now Alyson looked at him sideways.

The linens are white. The china is white. Everything you touch is white!

The singing got louder. He covered his ears.

The garbage smell got stronger. Now he was nauseous. He'd have to start cleaning soon.

If you start now you might never stop.

He grabbed the remote and turned on the widescreen television above the center island. He used to only watch the business channel. Now he surfed, hoping it would work like mental chemotherapy, save his mind by poisoning it.

He changed channels until he came to a young female anchor interviewing a middle-aged woman with narrow black glasses and short spiked hair. He named the interviewer Lee and the interviewee Spike. Lee's long red hair rolled down past her shoulders, and all her questions were nice and neat. Spike rambled on about men in mid-life crises as if she'd been one.

Jack hit the mute button. He couldn't listen but he couldn't stop watching.

The segment with Spike ended. The camera zoomed in on Lee. Her expression turned serious. She was telling a sad story, that much was clear even without the sound.

He squinted as he tried to read her lips. He blinked.

Alyson Walker appeared over Lee's left shoulder.

Jack froze.

He wanted to lunge for the remote and un-mute the sound, but he couldn't move. He was mesmerized—either by what was on the screen or by his mind messing with him, he didn't know which.

The segment ended. Lee and Alyson gave way to a commercial for baby wipes.

The garbage smell was gone. The children stopped singing.

He downed the last of his milk and looked back at the carton.

Have You Seen Her?

His heart rioted in his chest.

He had to find this Alyson, the one who got to be born. If he didn't, *he* was lost.

CHAPTER 5

JACK WAS IN HIS KITCHEN with the phone book open to the white pages on the center island. He flipped to the W's and squinted: two columns of Walkers. He started at the bottom of one column and worked backwards, his finger sliding up past William Walker to Joanne Walker, then over to the other column until his finger stopped at Alice Walker in Ridgewood. Alyson had last been seen in Ridgewood. Alice, Alyson—similar first names. Alice Walker had to be Alyson's mother.

Which meant Jack had to go to her house.

"Sorry to bother you," he said into the bedroom mirror, "but I think my dog ran into your yard. He got out of the car when I pulled over to make a call and headed that way."

Not bad.

But by the time he finished rehearsing and drove to Alice's house, she was pulling away in her red Fiat. He followed her to a strip mall, where she went into a dry cleaner's. She glanced in his direction before she made a call, then left with Jack on her tail. She proceeded to the Green Fields Market a few blocks away.

Health food. Susan shopped there sometimes. Jack sat in his car and watched the entrance for a minute. His thumbs tapped the steering wheel.

Finally he tossed his hat on the passenger seat, got out, and walked towards the market's entrance. The parking lot was half empty. He picked up his pace.

He wrangled a huge green shopping cart from the row of them lined up at the front of the store and pulled a disinfecting wipe from a dispenser near the carts.

A young man in front of him sneezed into his hand, which he used to steer his cart. Jack flinched, turned back, and yanked another wipe from the dispenser. After he wiped down his cart handle, he pulled out a third wipe for his hands.

You can't kill too many germs.

It was a hot day in July, but the air inside the store was so cold some female shoppers were wearing light jackets. Alice Walker hadn't been wearing one. She was thirtyish, blond, slender, and on the short side.

No surprise there.

Alyson and Susan both had fair skin and light blond hair. Both defied their age, but from opposite directions: Alyson was fifteen and looked twenty-five. Susan was thirty-five and looked twenty-five.

Jack kept glancing down the aisles, glad there weren't a lot of customers. In the frozen food aisle he saw a woman at the end reach into a freezer. Its door hid her face, but from her hair and petite figure he was sure she was Alice.

He pulled in a breath and pushed his cart towards her, moving past frozen yogurt and soy ice cream shelved behind tempered glass.

He'd start by asking her about whatever frozen food she'd selected. He tightened his tie and buttoned his blazer. He could do this.

Too many holes in that missing dog story anyway.

The woman still had her back to him when she stepped away from the freezer with something she needed both hands to carry. A giant box of veggie burgers? A gallon of peppermint ice cream?

"I've been meaning to try that," he said. "Is it any good?"

The woman—Alice!—spun around on red high heels.

"Nothing better." She held up a huge bag of frozen peas.

"Your daughter likes peas?"

"My daughter?" Now she looked directly at him.

"It was just a guess." He held up his hands.

"Who are you?" Her voice sounded hostile.

"I'm a neighbor." His sounded embarrassed.

"You." Her voice boomed. "I know who you are."

Jack tried to speak, but nothing came out. Alice's face zipped closed: eyes narrowed, lips pressed together in a thin line.

"Stay away from me."

"I was just trying to..." He took a step toward her, then stopped as a man with a crew cut appeared behind Alice. He was big, muscular, wearing khakis, a light blue polo shirt, and sunglasses. Jack named this character Mike.

"You causing a problem here?" Mike took off his sunglasses.

Is he on steroids?

"No problem." Jack showed them his palms and stepped back.

"He's stalking me," Alice said. "He was in front of my house this morning, then I saw him in the parking lot when I went to the dry cleaner's, and now he's here." She shook her head. "This world is full of crazies."

Jack's stomach churned.

"You're following her?" Mike put his sunglasses inside his jacket pocket and flexed his hand.

He's a Neanderthal.

"No—"

"So you're saying she's lying?"

"No!"

"Then you *are* a stalker."

Jack stepped backwards, rolling his cart with him, ready to use it to fend off this idiot. Mike stepped aside to make way for a shopper coming down the aisle. In the process he bumped against Alice's cart. As it rolled forward, its front wheel clipped her little toe.

"That hurt." Alice glared at Jack as if it were his fault.

"Sorry about your toe." Jack checked his watch. "But it looks like you're in good hands, and I've got to go." He spun his cart on its back wheels and pushed it away from them.

"Not so fast." Mike grabbed Jack's shoulder and turned him around.

"Are you a cop?" Jack asked. The guy looked like a cop.

"I don't know what you're up to," Mike said, "but you'd better stay away from her."

"I'm going now."

"Just make sure she never sees you again. We clear?"

Jack nodded and left. He tamped down his frustration. This had all made the next step that much harder.

CHAPTER 6

JACK ROLLED THE CHAIR away from his keyboard and pressed the pump on his hand sanitizer. A glob of the clear liquid plopped into his palm. He inhaled the alcohol as he rubbed his hands together.

Your writer's high.

It was 2:20 a.m. on a Tuesday, the room lit by the soft glow of the computer's monitor. Jack finished his second cup of coffee. There was a time when he never drank coffee before six a.m.— one of the many rules he'd lived by.

The back of his eyelids were sandpaper. He reeked of perspiration. He craved a hot shower, but that would have to wait.

He'd googled Alyson Walker, found one in Australia who'd published a cookbook at seventy-nine.

See, maybe it's not too late for you.

Another Alyson Walker had bowled two consecutive perfect games. She was fifty-two, African-American, and lived in Kentucky.

He snapped his fingers, rolled his chair back towards the

desk, and typed "Alice Walker Ridgewood" into Google's search box. He got three hits. His shoulders slumped when the first turned out to be the Alice he'd already followed. He kicked the flashback to yesterday's supermarket scene out of his head with a groan and looked at the second one, an Alice Walker who'd died in 1950 and was buried in the John Ridgewood cemetery in Atlanta. The third hit was a link to the website of Alice Walker, estate planner.

He sighed and clicked. A picture of the woman he'd followed filled his screen. She was in mid-sentence, standing next to an easel, pointing to the first of five bullet points.

A chill ran down his spine. He smacked his hands together and grabbed the mouse.

He clicked his way to Alice Walker's schedule and hit pay dirt: a one-day seminar at a Holiday Inn near Boston on July 10th at 9:00 a.m. Less than seven hours away.

He pumped out more hand sanitizer and worked it into his hands as his mind constructed a timeline.

Boston was a three-hour drive. He could get there before the seminar began, and this time he'd tell Alice the truth. It wouldn't take long to convince her that all he wanted was to help her find her daughter. He'd bring a picture of Susan and tell her about their Alison. He grabbed the rubber ball on his desk and started squeezing it, wishing he'd taken this approach to begin with. But he had to put that mistake behind him. He had to keep moving forward, making progress. He wouldn't make any more mistakes.

You better make damn sure of that.

After Boston there'd be a seminar in Vermont on Thursday and one in Maine on Friday.

Boston was the closest.

It was his best chance to meet Alice Walker. It would mean six hours of driving on a day when he'd slept only three hours the night before.

You can't miss this opportunity.

He went over the steps in his mind one by one. He nodded. Everything was falling into place. He'd lie down for a half-hour, then get ready to head to Boston.

Alice's website had directions to the hotel. It was right near the Thruway. He couldn't get lost even if he tried, and at the time he left there'd be little traffic.

He tented his fingers. He didn't know what to expect when he got there. He didn't know if there'd be thirty people at the seminar or three hundred. He didn't know if Alice would be at the front or back of the conference room waiting for the attendees to fill it or if she'd be behind closed doors until the seminar began. He figured the chances of this working out were fifty-fifty. Good enough odds—they'd have to be.

He just had to make sure he was back to meet Emily for lunch at one. He couldn't be late for that.

You've got to be on the road by nine-thirty.

He recalled the fury on Alice's face after the shopping cart ran over her toe. No stranger had ever been that angry at him before. So he'd change her opinion of him. He had plenty of money. She couldn't turn down his offer to help find her daughter.

He'd hire a private investigator if he had to, but what he really wanted to do was find Alyson himself. That was the only way he might get a taste of redemption.

Jack reached the Holiday Inn at 8:16.

He parked his car along the side of the hotel. He got out, shrugged into his suit jacket, and headed toward the hotel's entrance. He stepped through sliding glass doors and came to a sign that listed the events of the day.

Alice's seminar was in The Crystal Room.

Jack noticed a cluster of men and women in business casual attire standing by the elevator. Most looked young and eager.

Jack followed arrows to an attractive woman seated behind a table at the entrance to the Crystal Room. Her name badge said Sharon. She looked up at Jack and smiled.

He was about to speak when Alice Walker opened the door behind Sharon. She wore a navy blue suit and a white blouse.

"I can't get the projector to boot up—" She saw Jack. "What are you doing here?"

"I want to help you find your daughter." He was glad he'd taken this direct approach and pleased with the way his voice sounded: firm, filled with determination, making it clear he was someone she'd want helping her.

You're off to a good start.

"What are you talking about?" Alice said.

Sharon's smile slid from her face.

Alice balled up her hands.

Jack floundered.

"Alyson Walker, your missing daughter…I understand what it's like to lose someone you love—"

"I don't have a daughter."

"You're sure?" He peered at her, sweat breaking out on his upper lip.

"Leave right now or I'm calling security." She crossed her arms.

He closed his eyes. His shoulders felt heavy, his legs weak.

You fool. You should've known—no story resolves that easily.

He felt hot. He had to get out of there. He'd made another mistake and now he was back where he'd started.

You've lost time, precious time.

He turned away from the two women staring at him with expressions he couldn't read but knew would be burned on his brain.

He started back down the hall, trying to move as fast as he could, trying to steady himself. He watched the floor as he went around a corner—almost safe.

"Jack! What are you doing here?"

When he looked up, he saw Sean Sullivan walking towards him.

CHAPTER 7

SEAN STOPPED IN HIS TRACKS. He wore a red tie, striped shirt, dark suit.

Jack covered his face with his hands.

How twisted is this?

"You okay?" Sean came closer.

Jack's arms fell to his sides.

"I didn't get much sleep last night." He stepped back and shifted his eyes from left to right.

You're trapped.

"Are you going to this seminar too?" Sean pointed to a conference room. Above open double doors hung a banner that read: Be Afraid and Succeed.

"Why would I?" Jack's mind raced.

"Orson's seminars are amazing." Sean beamed. "You should go. This'll be my fourth. Each one has changed my life in a different way."

"I don't need anyone telling me how to live."

"Right." Sean looked down at the floor. "I called you yesterday. Did you get my message?"

"Guess I will when I get home." Jack rubbed his hands together. "One more reason to get there. Now if you'll excuse me, I need to eat."

"You mean breakfast? Mind if I join you?"

"What about Orson's seminar?" Jack glanced back at the banner. To him it looked like something stolen out of a high school gym. "I wouldn't want you to miss that."

Sean checked his watch. "It starts at ten." He pointed to the ceiling. "There's a restaurant upstairs. It's got decent food. And there's something important I have to tell you."

"Is this about work?"

"It is." Sean met Jack's gaze.

Jack couldn't imagine Sean saying anything important, but it was clear his partner wouldn't stop hounding him until he said it.

You might as well get this over with.

"Fine, let's do it." Jack tapped his foot. "I just have to be on the road by nine-thirty."

"No problem," Sean said.

"It better not be."

They rode the elevator in silence save for a bouncy tune with no discernible melody. Jack imagined a giant dentist drill, its gleaming bit buzzing. The image made his teeth ache, but Sean was whistling along to the Muzak. Jack wanted to stuff a handkerchief down his partner's throat. The elevator stopped, the doors parted, and they stepped into the lobby.

"I need to use the restroom." Washing his hands would calm him.

"I'll be here." Sean's eyes followed a young woman in a tight dress.

Jack walked past the reception desk and a door with a

silhouette of a bonnet, then on to a door with a silhouette of a top hat.

"Why can't they just say Men?" Jack muttered as he entered the brightly lit bathroom. He looked around, checked under the stalls. No shoes. "At least you're alone and the place is clean."

He stepped in front of a sink, opened the spigot, and pumped a glob of soap into his palm. It smelled like coconut. His breathing slowed as he worked the lather through his fingers. He closed his eyes. He was at the beach, in Jamaica, the tide going out, the white sand warm to his bare feet. Seagulls cried as gentle waves broke against the shore. Susan was walking towards him in a white bikini, coming out of the ocean, her hair wet, her fair skin glistening in the bright, bright sun.

She was about to speak when the bathroom door banged open. Someone scurried into a stall.

"What?" Jack whispered. "Susan, tell me." But she was gone. Jack opened his eyes.

Discourteous bastard.

He rinsed his hands and dried them under the blower. He grabbed the door handle to leave. It was wet, slimy. He shivered. He recalled the pig who sneezed into his palm at the supermarket yesterday.

Bastards and pigs.

He washed his hands again and used a paper towel to open the door.

When Jack returned to the lobby he found Sean in a thick oversized chair—legs crossed, arms folded over his chest, a wave of light brown hair falling across his high forehead. His eyes weren't quite closed, but Jack looked around for the nearest exit. Sean bolted from the chair.

"Let's go. I'm hungry." He started to put his arm around Jack, who slipped out of range so fast Sean let the arm drop as though he had no idea what it had been up to.

Rich Silvers

The middle-aged woman who greeted them as they entered the restaurant smiled at Sean and led them past framed photographs of the Pantheon, the Eiffel Tower, and the Coliseum to a table near the back of the room.

A hefty waitress came over brandishing a pot of coffee in each hand—one had a green lid, the other orange. Her nametag read Bernice.

Jack asked for regular and turned his coffee cup over.

Sean left his upside down and ran a palm over it as if staying pat in blackjack.

"You stopped drinking coffee?" Jack asked. Sean had always claimed he was useless before his first cup.

"I have so much more energy without that stuff." Sean looked at Jack's steaming black coffee as if it had mold growing on it. "Gave it up after the Live Healthy seminar."

"You quit drinking alcohol too?"

"Making positive changes is about balance. I still enjoy my Grey Goose every now and then."

Jack looked at him sideways. "Only now and then?"

His partner blushed and sipped some ice water. He'd once told Jack, "I drink on Monday to start the week, Wednesday to get through the middle, and Friday and Saturday because it's over."

"I couldn't keep living that way." Sean looked at his hands. "Besides, now that I'm running things all by myself, I can't slack off."

"Work's taking a toll on you?" Jack said through his teeth, recalling the many times he'd covered for Sean.

"Actually, it's keeping me sane."

He used to claim work drove him nuts.

Bernice returned and pulled out a pad.

"I'll have oatmeal with blueberries." Sean looked up from the menu and gave her a politician's smile. "And please make sure the blueberries are fresh."

The crap he used to put in his body and now he's worried about fresh blueberries.

Bernice scribbled a few letters.

Jack cracked his knuckles.

"Give me scrambled eggs, toast, and bacon. Oh, and I'll have a small fresh-squeezed orange juice."

"Sorry, we only have concentrate." Bernice stopped writing.

"I'll have that," Jack said.

"I'll have the juice too," Sean said.

"Careful, it's not fresh-squeezed."

"Juice, please."

"Shake it up and it'll taste more like fresh," Jack said.

Sean looked around as soon as Bernice left and whispered, "You didn't have to make a scene."

"Why not? I'm getting good at them." Jack threaded his hands together, palms out, and stretched his arms.

"What are you talking about?"

"Never mind." Jack waved him off. "You're not reading it."

Sean spread his fingers flat on the table. The tip of one grazed Jack's fork.

Jack recalled the time Sean had left the restroom without washing his hands. He couldn't eat with that fork.

"So how are you doing?" Sean asked, oblivious to what his finger had just done.

Jack felt Sean's eyes on him as he kept his on the placemat's advertisements. Oil Change While U Wait. Call Lenny: No Job Too Small.

"You're not going to talk to me?" Sean said.

"There's a coupon here for a free car wash." Jack pointed to the middle of the placemat. "And did you know you can refinance your mortgage at a great rate?"

"Jack."

"Sean, we're business partners, not best buddies. Surely you know that."

"And whose fault is—"

Jack held up his hands. "I'll take full responsibility as long as things don't change."

"Now you're being silly."

Jack sipped his coffee. Some rolled down his chin. He grabbed his napkin off his lap to wipe it, but a good sized drop fell onto his pants, next to his fly.

Shit.

He wet the napkin and blotted the stain. That left a larger mark.

Sean straightened a teaspoon.

Jack eyed the stain.

He's a jinx.

"So when are you coming back to work?" Sean adjusted his water glass as if it were an intricate procedure.

"You miss me?" Jack peered in at him.

"Our clients are asking about you." Logan & Sullivan managed money, very successfully, for a group of wealthy investors. The partnership consistently exceeded the market's averages.

"Tell them I'm on sabbatical."

"But you're coming back after that." Sean's finger was about to graze Jack's teaspoon. Jack moved it just in time.

"I'm not sure." Jack turned and saw Bernice taking an order from six foreign businessmen. None seemed to speak English. It was like they were playing charades. "I might never come back."

"I can't imagine what you must be going through, but I would think getting back to work would be therapeutic."

Jack snapped his fingers and pointed at Sean. "I bet Orson taught you that at the second seminar. What was that one called?"

"You can be negative, Jack. A little positive influence in your life might do you good." Sean held up his hand as Jack was about to speak. "Forget about that. The bottom line is, you know it takes two to run our shop right."

"You'll just have to soldier on without me. Hire a temp." Jack's stomach growled. Bernice was only on the second businessman. He wished someone could take over for her so she could check on their order.

"You expect me to continue without any idea as to when or if you're coming back?"

"It's none of your business."

"Bullshit."

"Surprised you still curse. Thought Orson would've had you give that up in the third seminar."

"How would you feel if I left and didn't say whether I'd be back?"

"Hallelujah!" Jack stood up and raised his arms, shaking his hands.

"You're embarrassing yourself, Jack. You're my partner. I have the right to know what's going on."

Jack sat back down.

"I'm searching for someone, okay?"

"Who? Why?" Sean looked intrigued.

"Someone who's missing."

Jack winced as he heard Alice's voice in his head: *I don't have a daughter.*

"Why don't you hire a professional?" Sean asked.

"I'm choosing not to handle it that way so far."

"That's not like you, Jack. You always say, 'Get the best.' That's your solution to everything."

"Too bad I didn't do that when I chose a partner."

"You're ungrateful."

"I should be grateful for you?"

"Don't change the subject, you're not *interested* in me. Why aren't you hiring someone to find this missing person?"

"I'm trying something different." Jack was going to pass out if the damn food didn't come soon.

"Is this someone you're related to?"

"No."

"Then who is it?" Sean's finger neared Jack's fork again. Jack didn't care. He wouldn't be using it.

Bernice was stuck on the last businessman. Jack wanted to yell, 'Is there an interpreter in the house?'

A waitress appeared with a nametag that read Donna and a plate in each hand.

"Who's having the lox and bagel?" she asked.

"I'll take it," Jack said.

"And you're having the Belgian waffle?" Donna turned to Sean.

"Actually, we didn't order either of these things," Sean said.

"Oh. I'm sorry—"

"Give me that damn bagel." Jack went after it with both hands.

"This isn't your order." Donna pulled the plate away from him. "What's wrong with you?"

"I'm *hungry*. This is a restaurant, isn't it? People are supposed to eat here, aren't they?"

"We're really busy. Your food will be out shortly."

"That's what you all say."

Donna walked to a table where a man and woman were holding up their hands like kids in a school room.

Bernice was finally finishing up. Jack willed her to the kitchen.

"Come back to work," Sean said. "You owe it to our clients."

"Didn't you have something important to tell me?"

Sean's face went into thinking mode: brow wrinkled, lips pursed. Finally he lifted his chin.

"Marjorie's leaving."

"What?" The revelation felt like a slap. He'd have expected Marjorie to tell him herself. After all, he'd do anything for her—

But she'd come to see him Sunday and he pushed her away. She must have wanted to tell him then.

You never gave her a chance.

"She gave a month's notice," Sean said. "But if you come back, I think she'll stay."

"What did you do?" He lunged for Sean, the table held him back. "Son of a bitch, tell me what did you did."

"Nothing," Sean showed Jack his palms. "She says her reasons are personal. I pressed her, but she wanted to talk to you."

"If I find out you did anything—" Jack balled his hands.

"You need to talk to her, Jack."

"I will."

Bernice returned with a tray over her shoulder. She blew out a breath, checked her order pad, and set a bowl of oatmeal in front of Sean.

Jack dropped his fork on the floor just as she set down his plate. She plucked another off an empty table and handed it to him.

You should give her a good tip.

Jack doused his eggs with ketchup, knowing Sean found the combination disgusting.

And that's when he didn't care about what he ate.

"What do you have against me?" Sean asked.

"You're not thorough and sometimes you're greedy."

Sean nodded as if he expected Jack to say that.

"And I can't trust you." Jack stared at Sean.

"So I'm a spoiled, lazy, rich kid, right?"

"Bingo." Jack didn't believe people made lasting changes, at least not for the better.

"I know," Sean raised his hands as if quieting a crowd, "you grew up poor and your parents got divorced, and I'm supposed to feel guilty because—"

"This isn't about me. It's about you." Jack buttered his toast. He was hungry, ravenous. Sean had yet to touch his oatmeal. He'd better get going or Jack would eat that, too.

"What about the last three months?" Sean used his spoon

to arrange the blueberries in a symmetrical pattern on top of his oatmeal. "You see what I've done on my own. How do you explain that?"

"You know what they say about not confusing brains with a bull market." Jack folded half a slice of toast and ate it in two bites. Then he ate the other half.

"You can't write it all off to just that."

"Keep it up, then I'll believe it." Jack downed the last of his orange juice, slapped the glass down on the table, and sighed with pleasure. "I just better not get a call from the SEC."

"Come on, Jack, you really think I'd do something illegal?"

"Greed distorts your judgment. That's when you get dangerous, and now I'm not there to keep an eye on you." Soon Marjorie wouldn't be either.

"I'm not that way anymore." Sean sprinkled brown sugar on his oatmeal.

Jack chewed a chunk of scrambled egg. *A little less ketchup next time.*

Sean held a spoonful of oatmeal, a blueberry on top, his hand shaking.

"I admit there were times when I got anxious and took shortcuts, but now I have the discipline to apply what you taught me."

Jack, too, had been anxious when he first started trading, desperate to prove he could make it on his own. He, too, had taken shortcuts. They had cost him a lot of money.

"Let me guess," Jack said. "It's Orson's seminars that gave you this discipline."

Sean aligned the salt and pepper shakers, studied them as if to make sure they were just right.

"They helped, but the real change came that last day you were at work."

"How?" Jack cocked an eyebrow.

"I delayed you. I'm partly responsible for what happened."

Sean finally looked up from the shakers. "It's something I've needed to tell you."

Jack sat back in his seat. He'd gone back to that day thousands of times. True, if Sean hadn't been greedy that day, Jack wouldn't have kept debating with him, wouldn't have been late. But in the end he always came to the same conclusion.

It's your fault and only your fault.

Jack couldn't see it any other way.

"Wanting to keep that stock was a stupid gamble and if I hadn't argued with you your wife would probably still be alive." Sean sucked in a breath and let it out slowly. "I think about that a lot." He centered his bowl of oatmeal on the placemat. "I'll never be reckless again."

Blood rushed to Jack's face. "So you're telling me your guilt from what happened that day has given you the discipline to be successful?"

"Yes." Sean looked as if he had just grasped the meaning of life.

Why was it so warm? Jack ran a finger under his shirt collar. Damp.

"So you've taken this guilt, guilt you don't have a right to, and turned it into something positive for yourself? And now you expect me to feel, what? Proud of you? Sorry for you?"

"No, I wanted you to—"

"Come on, Sean. It's easy for you to blame yourself for Susan's death. Wait, let me correct myself. You're only partly to blame, right?"

"Well, I—"

"But we both know who's really to blame." He stabbed himself with his thumb. "Me! I bet people tell you, 'Sean you shouldn't feel that way' and deep down you know you don't have to. Deep down you know one day you won't. It'll all be in the past, like the time you got so drunk at Marjorie's Christmas party you pissed in your pants!"

"I didn't mean to imply—"

"Shut up, I see it now. You'll tell Orson to use it in one of his seminars." He drew a banner in the air. "Make guilt work for you." His voice got louder. "How much will he charge for that?" Jack grabbed the sides of the table and leaned forward, spittle on his lips. "That's the difference between you and me, Sean. This isn't just some mistake I can capitalize on. This is my life. And I want you to stay out of it."

"Jack, you're taking this the wrong way." Sean spread his arms.

"Do you hear me, Sean? Stay the hell out of my life!"

"I don't need to sit here and listen to your insults." Sean stood up and threw his napkin on the table.

"You're leaving before you finish your oatmeal?" Jack's heart pounded, his shirt was soaked.

"I know you're in a lot of pain, Jack. And I forgive you."

Jack gave him the finger. Sean left.

Jack speared a chunk of egg, but he couldn't eat anymore. His stomach was a knot. He put down his fork, caught Bernice's eye, and tapped his palm.

Figures you'd get stuck with the bill.

Jack entered the lobby and sank into the chair Sean had sat in earlier. His hands were shaking. He had a three-hour drive ahead of him. He put his head back on the thick cushion. The anger rumbling inside him gave way to exhaustion. He closed his eyes.

When he woke, the lobby was empty. He looked at his watch. It was almost ten. He should have been on the road a half-hour ago.

CHAPTER 8

DANIELA'S WAS IN A STRIP MALL but it had an upscale décor: walnut paneling, brass light fixtures, big comfortable chairs with armrests.

Jack stood looking for Emily at one-twenty—out of breath because he'd run from his car. He was sure she'd gotten there at one. Not a minute before or after. Getting there early would suggest anxiety; getting there late, disorganization.

He was about to walk past a sign that said Please Wait to be Seated when a tall slender hostess with Mediterranean skin came over to him.

"Do you have a reservation?"

"I'm meeting Emily White."

He'd forgotten his cell phone that morning, but he made good time driving back from Boston and had felt confident he'd be there by one. And he would have had construction not slowed traffic to a single lane ten minutes from Daniela's. Sitting in his car stuck in traffic made Jack sweat like nothing else on earth. Restaurants didn't have showers, and he needed one badly. He was still sweating.

"Please follow me," the hostess said.

He walked behind her, passing restaurant patrons, picking up bits of their inane conversations. He needed silence. He needed to be alone. He'd get neither one here.

He wanted to ask the hostess to speed up, but one woman in this restaurant pissed off at him was enough.

Wait a minute—the hostess was wearing Eternity, Susan's perfume.

Suddenly his wife's face was everywhere, plastered on the bearded man to his right *and* on the skinny woman laughing to his left. The images were distorted, but the characteristics of these strangers' faces somehow resembled Susan.

How'd they do that?

Jack blinked.

The Susan faces were still there. He was dizzy. But he kept moving.

Sinatra's "Summer Wind" seeped through the air like a fog settling on an unsuspecting night. It was one of Susan's favorite songs, though she could take or leave the artist. "Chairman of the Board, a bit pretentious wouldn't you say?" Even as Jack recalled her saying this, he saw her arched eyebrow on the face of a young man. "But it's a wonderful song!" she'd add.

You've got to get out of here!

He saw himself bolting for the door, crashing into tables along the way as silverware clanged, glasses crashed, and liquids spilled in his wake.

He was about to submit to this urge when an overweight Susan/woman shouted at a Susan-faced boy jumping up and down. "Don't."

The Susan faces vanished.

The hostess stopped next to a booth with a table that had

ferns dangling above it and Emily seated on one side in a sophisticated black dress.

"Glad you could make it." She took a long sip from her martini glass.

"Sorry I'm late." He slid into the booth, noticing the coffee stain on his pants from breakfast with Sean.

Damn.

He plucked a red cloth napkin from a crystal tumbler and placed it on his lap.

"No need to explain," Emily wore her long red hair pulled back with a few tendrils around a very lovely face. At forty she looked better than she ever had.

"Our house wine is a Montepulciano," the hostess said as she handed Jack a heavy menu. "Would you like a glass?"

"I need something with a bite," Jack said. "Give me a Shiraz."

"And I'll have another dirty martini." Emily downed the rest of her drink and handed the empty glass to the hostess.

"I just came from Boston. I had breakfast with my partner. I got stuck in a traffic jam on the way back." Jack swallowed. "They'd have to give me a lobotomy before I'd do that again."

You'd better watch what you say.

Emily checked her nails. They were short and clear with French tips.

"You have so many talents, Jack Logan. Too bad punctuality isn't one of them."

"Don't go there, Emily."

"That a threat?" Anger seeped into her green eyes.

Jack looked away and saw a man tugging on the arm of a little girl. She was crying, wriggling, trying to escape. But the man's grip was too strong. The girl's arm was turning red. No one in the restaurant seemed to notice what was happening right before their very eyes. Jack had to do something. He had to stop this girl from being abducted. A crime was being committed in broad daylight.

He blinked.

The girl was laughing. She hugged the man and called him Daddy.

"It's always about you, Jack," Emily said. "That's your problem."

Jack hit his head with the heel of his hand.

"What's wrong?" Emily appeared perplexed.

"This is playing out way too weird."

"What are you talking about?" She leaned closer.

"Never mind, you're not reading it either."

"Jack?"

"Look, just stop breaking my balls about being late."

"You think I wanted to?" Emily asked.

"I think you were looking for the opportunity."

"You're an idiot if you think that."

"What else do I have to go on?"

"How about the fact I'm still here." She looked out the window. "If I wanted to make a point, I'd have left. You should've called."

"I forgot my cell phone."

"And I bet your dog ate your homework."

He grabbed the sides of the table. "I was STUCK IN TRAFFIC! My worst nightmare. How many times do I have to tell you?"

"And there were no pay phones anywhere. What a primitive society we live in!"

"They don't have pay phones in the middle of traffic jams, Emily. You can't move in the middle of a traffic jam. That's why they call it a jam. Now do you need my help or did you invite me to lunch to make me feel even worse than I already feel?"

Emily rubbed her arms. The restaurant was cool. The air conditioning must've been turned up all the way. Jack was still sweating, dirty. He snuck out the bottle of sanitizer. It fell on the floor.

Jack closed his eyes and tried to find his composure. It had to be there somewhere.

A waitress came over with their drinks.

"I'm Maria," she said.

"We're not ready to order," Emily said. The waitress smiled and left.

Jack stared at his glass but couldn't reach for it. He saw himself pounding the table. The liquids in the glasses swaying. Wine spilling on the table cloth. He wanted to clean it up.

"Is something bothering you?" Emily asked.

He stared at her, unsure of her sincerity.

Emily slid out of the booth and walked past him, then turned around.

"I'll be back." She had a hand on her hip, a bracelet dangled on her wrist. "Maybe my absence will calm you down." She went toward the ladies room.

Jack bent down and picked up the sanitizer. He rubbed some into his hands. He felt calmer. He gazed out the window on his left.

A teenage girl in baggy pants and a dirty white tee shirt was coming toward him. Her arms were pencil thin and her blond hair was cut short. She moved quickly, head down, hands in her pockets.

He blinked. The girl was still there.

She's real, Logan. Get a grip.

Finding Alyson seemed daunting—even more so after his failure this morning. He needed help. He felt alone.

What happens next?

Finally he was able to take a sip of wine.

You need to figure that out.

When Emily slipped back into the booth he smelled perfume. He hadn't before. She flipped through the menu.

"I'm having steak." She looked at him. "You know what you want?"

"You mean to eat?"

Emily smiled.

"Think I'll try the chicken cacciatore." He sipped more of the wine. It bit the back of his throat. He took another sip.

"Don't worry, Jack, I'll tell you what this is about." Emily folded her reading glasses and beckoned Maria.

"I'll have the New York Strip," she said. "And tell the chef I want it very rare."

"Sorry, we can't go lower than medium rare." Maria's eyes met Emily's. "But medium here is *really* rare."

"It's not complicated, just take the steak off the fire a little sooner." Emily's tone bordered on hostile.

Jack was relieved he wasn't the focus of her frustration—any minute now she'd be asking to see the manager.

"Just do the best you can," she said.

"Of course," Maria said and got the hell out of Dodge.

"I did that for you," Emily said.

"And I thought you were getting mellow."

"No way." Emily smirked.

"You haven't changed."

"Is there a reason to?"

The hostess passed by, seating a young couple two tables down from them. She smiled at Jack as she strutted back to her podium.

"Seems you've made a good first impression." Emily stirred her drink and nodded her head to where the hostess had just been. "Question is: can you keep it?"

"No way."

Emily laughed and raised her drink. "Touché, Mr. Logan." Their glasses clinked. Emily took a long sip of her drink. "I used to meet Susan here on Wednesdays." Another sip.

Jack knew Susan had secrets. Now he knew lunches with Emily was one of them.

At Susan's funeral Emily had held up better than most, but

now her eyes were teary and her voice not quite steady. Her glass already two-thirds empty.

"I loved Susan," she said. "We were getting closer just before she died."

He sat on his hands.

"Susan loved you, Jack. You didn't always make it easy for her. But don't be too hard on yourself. Susan wasn't as perfect as people believed."

Confusion rumbled inside him.

"You seem surprised." Emily reached for her water, almost knocking over his wine glass in the process. She caught it just in time. Her fingers wrapped its rim as she moved it off to the side. He stared at it, knowing he couldn't drink from it now.

Susan wasn't as perfect as people believed. The words gnawed at him.

"I thought you were going to tell me why I'm here," he said. "This scene is running long and I have no idea what you want."

She gave him an odd look, then finished her drink.

"Money."

"You want *money*?"

"Fifty thousand." Emily held his gaze.

"You want me to lend you fifty thousand dollars?" He moved his eyes from side to side. "Of course you do."

Emily nodded.

It didn't make sense. Emily sold high-end real estate and last he knew she was still doing well despite the pop in the real estate bubble.

Silence.

This should be when she said why she needed the money. But he knew she wouldn't.

"Stop by the house on Friday. I'll give you a check." He waited for her to add a complication—she needed the money sooner, or only cash would do. He expected her to thank him. He expected her to look at him. Something.

But she just turned toward the window, her perfect profile reflecting off the glass.

CHAPTER 9

SUSAN WASN'T AS PERFECT as people believed.

Jack shivered behind the wheel, driving home from Daniela's.

Why would Emily say that about his wife—her sister?

You should've confronted her about it when you had the chance.

Maybe their being half-sisters was the reason. Maybe Emily was jealous. Maybe that was why she was such a bitch.

His anger was a ball in the center of his chest—wrapped tight, getting tighter.

He recalled Emily's tapping her stirrer on the edge of her glass as she said it, eyes locked on his. It wasn't something she'd regret saying later on. No. It was delivered sharply, precisely, like a surgeon making an incision.

Where are all the cars?

The tree-lined streets were quiet, houses tucked away behind elaborate landscaping. No traffic.

He had the radio on, "Moon River." He and Susan had once

danced to it cheek to cheek, his arms tight around her, her body close, her delicate scent the only thing he ever wanted to—

A blue ball rolled into the street. A little girl appeared in front of Jack's car.

He slammed on the brakes. The car jerked to an abrupt stop. He was flung forward to the seatbelt's limit.

A young woman ran after the girl, horror on her face. The little girl picked up the ball, smiling. The woman glared at Jack as she grabbed the girl's hand and led her back to the sidewalk.

He let out a deep breath and continued forward at a crawl, peering out his windshield, recalling that little girl running in front of his car. Suddenly the music was too loud. His head pounded.

He missed a turn and tried a shortcut that should lead him to Brandon Way, a side road near his house. It led him into a cul-de-sac. A sign read Children at Play. But the streets were empty.

Is everyone on vacation?

He turned right, going back the way he came. Ten minutes later, he was in the cul-de-sac again.

You're lost.

The air conditioner was on high, but he was hot. The sun beat down on the hood of his car. He opened the window. The air was still and thick, tinged with a faint scent of skunk.

Susan wasn't as perfect as people believed.

He stopped the car and covered his ears.

SUSAN WASN'T AS PERFECT AS PEOPLE BELIEVED!

He'd been up since two. He needed to shower. He needed sleep. But he had to prove Emily wrong before he did anything else.

You have to find your way home first.

He drove, squinting as he read small green street signs—Poplar Way, Poplar Drive, Poplar Court. He was in a development. The houses were raised ranches, every one painted white. An old woman was in her front yard, had a kind face under her wide straw hat. Just as he was about to pull over and ask for directions she turned and went inside. He continued on. Poplar Terrace, Poplar Avenue—

He was an idiot. He had GPS.

He turned it on and set it for home. The lady—he'd named her Cynthia—said, "At the next intersection, make a right turn." He did. After another block she said, "At the next intersection, make a left turn." He turned left and kept going, awaiting Cynthia's next prompt.

"Susan wasn't as perfect as people believed," she said.

His car screeched to a halt. Jack looked at the screen: "Recalculating."

He put the car in park and buried his face in his hands.

There was a knock on the window.

He looked up to see a young girl holding a skateboard. He pushed a button and the window fell away.

"You all right, Mr. Logan?" The girl looked vaguely familiar.

Jack nodded and looked around. He was in front of his house.

How long have you been here?

He pressed the accelerator. The engine roared but the car didn't move.

It's in park, you idiot.

He shifted into drive and pulled into his garage, where he sat. And sat.

He got out of the car finally and went down the driveway. The sun was bright, the heat still relentless at four p.m.

"Hey, Jack," Fred said as he made his way toward Jack's mailbox. "I've been meaning to ask you…"

Jack held up a hand.

"Sorry, can't talk now." He grabbed the mail, hurried back into his house, locked the door, and dropped the mail on the center island. He picked up the first envelope, the credit card bill, slid a letter opener under its flap.

Wait, what are you doing?

He didn't have time for this. He put down the envelope and stepped back from the center island. The floor was unsteady. *He* was unsteady.

He grabbed the phone and dialed Emily's number. Words formed in his mind. Things he had to get off his chest. He jabbed the buttons harder. She'd better apologize. His finger froze.

You need more than words.

He needed physical proof. Something he could shove in her face. That was the only way to convince Emily she was wrong. The proof had to be somewhere in this house.

IT HAS TO BE!

Jack loosened his tie, staggered into the living room, and fell onto the couch.

He needed to think. He needed a plan. He needed to do something right.

Jack woke in darkness. He felt calm. Then his mind started racing.

He got up from the couch and opened the blinds. Dusk slipped in from the picture window. He'd been asleep for nearly five hours.

He started pacing.

Susan was sitting on the loveseat in a white nightgown, her hands folded in her lap. She looked up at him. "Why is Emily saying those things about me?"

"I don't know."

"Help me, Jack." Pain was on her face.

"I will."

He ran upstairs, turned left, and stopped at the master bedroom. He hadn't been in that room since Susan died. He took a deep breath and went in.

Susan's smock was sprawled out on the bed, right where she'd left it.

"Mind putting that away for me?" she asked.

Jack felt her breath on the back of his neck. His hands hovered over the smock.

You can't touch it.

He inhaled and smelled dirty laundry. He looked down at the wicker hamper in front of the bed. Those clothes had been in there for three months.

"They stink. Wash them, Jack."

He couldn't touch them, either. He turned away from the hamper.

You're too dirty.

He saw his reflection in the mirrored doors on Susan's closet. He stepped back until his image vanished.

Two club chairs sat in front of French doors that led to the balcony. Susan sat in the chair on the right, under the moon. She had on the black blouse he'd given her. The one she had on when she died.

He wiped away a tear. "You're wrong about her, Emily!" he screamed.

You still need proof.

Now Susan was lying on the bed—ankles crossed, head propped up by a pillow. She was reading a book: *One Hundred Things to Do before You Die.* His wife once said she had such a list. He'd planned to ask if he could see it but never got around to it. Some of the things on that list had to be about helping others—maybe all of them.

You're the reason she didn't do them.

He had to find that list. He had to show it to Emily, watch her read it, and wait for her expression to say she was wrong. The list had to be in this house.

He looked around. Could it be in this room? The hairs on his arms rose.

Susan lowered the book, smiled, and pointed to the ceiling. Then she was gone.

Jack pulled down the folding staircase that led to the attic. He'd lived in this house for two years and had never been up there. He flipped on a light switch and looked up. He ascended the stairs, gripping the steps above him, his legs wobbly but at least they got him to the top. The air smelled musty.

The attic was empty except for a white desk and a matching chair. They sat against the far wall, under the air vent. It was Susan's desk, the one she'd used before they were married. He had surprised her with a large oak one when they moved into this house, but she looked almost disappointed after he removed his hands from her eyes to show her the present he spent weeks searching for. She never explained her reaction. He never asked.

You should have.

He walked towards the desk, stepping lightly as if he might scare it away.

"Sit," he heard Susan say. He sat.

He slid out the desk's middle drawer. It was packed with office supplies in disarray. He smiled wistfully. Even Susan had a junk drawer.

He tried opening the two side drawers. They didn't budge. His fingers felt the lock on the inside panel of the desk. He searched the middle drawer but didn't find a key.

The attic was well insulated. It had to be ninety degrees up here. He wiped his sweaty forehead with a forearm.

An image popped into his head.

He went downstairs and into the first-floor study. He sat at the desk he'd bought Susan and opened its middle drawer. It, too, had office supplies, though here they were neatly arranged. He pulled the drawer all the way out and found a small white leather pouch lying at the back. Inside the pouch was a skeleton key. It was solid, heavy for its size. He tossed it in the air and caught it in his palm.

Back in the attic, he slipped the key into the desk's lock and turned it. He heard the latch release. His heart raced as he opened the top side drawer. He found files from the grade school classes Susan had taught before they were married. In the bottom drawer he found more files. One was labeled Finances, another Credit Card Bills, and another Open Items. His finger flicked the plastic tabs until it stopped at Someday/Maybe. He removed that file and used the one behind it to mark its place.

He opened Someday/Maybe flat on the desk and saw an ad for hot yoga classes. Next was an article on the benefits of wheat grass. There was a business card from a psychic named Sasha May. He memorized the phone number and dealt the card off to the side.

An envelope was the last thing in the folder. His hands shook as he removed a piece of paper folded in thirds.

Could this be the list?

He unfolded it and read it.

A,

They say sometimes writing a letter to someone can help you cope with what you're feeling toward them—even if you don't send it. I'm feeling so many things right now. So I'm writing this letter to you.

I haven't stopped thinking about you since the last time I held you. Yes, it was a long time ago, and one would think time would dissipate one's feelings, but that hasn't happened with me.

No, time has only made them grow stronger in ways I never could've expected. And now that I have someone who's supposed to take your place, I realize no one can. That fact burns deep in my soul.

Once I believed being apart was best for both of us. Now I no longer do. I hope you feel the same. I know it's selfish for me to want that after what I did to you, but it's something I can no longer deny.

I love you. Always have, always will. I was young and thought I couldn't give you what you needed. Now I know all you needed was love. And because of my failure to realize this, we now have separate lives. I've tried, but I can't figure out a way to change that without hurting people who don't deserve to be hurt.

I realize I've caused you pain. Some in ways I'll never know. Please forgive me and believe that I will always love you and will always regret what I did.

Jack put the letter on top of the desk and stared at the far wall. His face felt flushed. His mind lived to play tricks on him. This couldn't be right, couldn't be real.

But when he looked down at the top of the desk, the letter was still there.

And when he picked it up and studied the neat, rounded penmanship, with Susan's unmistakable loops, he had no doubt that she wrote it.

Could he have misinterpreted the content? Was there was a nuance he hadn't picked up on?

He read the letter again. Susan's melodic voice played inside his head. When he got to the end, he was sure of two things: it was written to someone his wife loved and it wasn't him.

He sat motionless, waiting for anger to boil. It didn't. If anything he loved his wife more.

It was addressed to A.

That had to be Alan Dean.

Susan had told him about Alan the morning after their first

night together, right after she revealed her fear of driving in the city.

Alan was her first love; she'd hoped he'd be her last. But the relationship didn't work out—Susan had been vague about why and Jack hadn't asked. He just held on to the tenderness in her eyes when she told him that now she was glad it hadn't.

"This is my fault," he said through his teeth.

It was useless, so useless. Nothing could change what he had done, or in his case what he hadn't done. He married a goddess, found her when he thought he never would. All he had to do was love her the way she deserved—

You're pathetic.

His hands shook as he slid the letter back in the envelope and put the file away. He locked the drawers and went down the attic stairs.

Find Alyson. It's all you have left.

Jack stepped into the shower. He opened the spigot and turned the spray to needle. Pins of hot water stung him. Steam rose.

He was in a fog, screaming his wife's name inside his brain without making a sound. He stayed like that until the water turned cold, then shut it off. He leaned against the tiles and slid down and sat on the floor.

He wanted to cry but he couldn't. He wanted to let go of his need to find Alyson Walker but he couldn't do that, either. Maybe he still needed to punish himself, or maybe he just needed something to focus on. He didn't know which. The only thing he did know was what he'd do next.

CHAPTER 10

SASHA MAY LIVED IN A TINY HOUSE in a neighborhood Jack normally avoided like a handshake from someone with a runny nose.

He sat in Sasha's living room, which barely had room to accommodate a loveseat, chair, and end table. He wondered if his fifty-thousand-dollar sports car would still be where he parked it when he left. In the same pristine condition. He got up and was looking out the window at it when he heard steps.

"Mr. Logan." Sasha stood in the doorway. "I'm ready to see you now."

He'd expected her to be wearing a long black dress, not faded blue jeans and a gray sweatshirt with its sleeves pushed up past her elbows. She was small and chubby with circles under her eyes. Maybe guilt from selling false hope kept her up nights.

"There's no need to worry about your car." She'd caught him peeking through her blinds like a convict on the run. "My son, Anthony, is home today. He'll keep an eye on it for you."

Did she wink?

Jack checked the window again and saw a long-haired teenage boy wearing headphones and dressed all in black. His head bobbed as he crossed his arms and leaned against Jack's car.

Jack released the blinds.

Sasha smiled.

Had Susan been here?

Jack followed Sasha down a dim, narrow hallway. She stopped and opened a door. "Please have a seat on the left."

He stepped into a room no bigger than a closet and sat at a round marble table.

"I'll be right back." The psychic left before he could ask how long she'd be. He heard a click, then he was alone.

He could hear muffled voices on the other side of the door. Neither sounded like a woman's. He leaned closer, heard laughter, then nothing.

Jack felt warm, but he kept his suit jacket on and didn't loosen his tie. He stared at the gold doorknob to his right.

You think it's locked?

The room was white, its walls bare. A tall, thin, red box sat on the table next to a button that resembled a doorbell. Beside the box was a brass clock, ticking out the seconds of his life.

Jack caught a faint whiff of incense. It made him nauseous. He checked his watch. He'd been in this prison cell for five minutes. He'd find Sasha and tell her he needed to use the restroom.

That's assuming you can get out.

The doorknob turned just as Jack reached for it. His hand jumped back as if it had been burned.

Sasha stepped into the room and sat down across from his chair.

"Sorry for the delay." She pushed up her sleeves. They fell back down. "You've been to a psychic before?" Her dark eyes slid toward the clock and then back to him.

"I don't believe..." He wiped sweat from his upper lip. "I think my wife came here."

"She's no longer with us?" Sasha raised her thick eyebrows.

"How did you know that?" Jack's leg was shaking. "Who are you?"

"It was only a guess, Mr. Logan. Most people who come here have just lost someone they love. Please accept my condolences." She put her clasped hands on the table. Silver rings were on all of her thick fingers, even her thumbs. "I charge forty dollars for a reading. I work by touch. Give me your hands and I'll tell you what I can."

"No." Jack dug his nails into his thighs. He couldn't have physical contact with this woman.

Sasha's face was immobile. Waiting.

"I just need to know if..." He reached into his jacket pocket, pulled out a picture of Susan, and showed it to Sasha. "This is my wife. Has she been here?"

Sasha reached for the picture.

Jack wouldn't let go.

"She came here, yes," Sasha said.

He shifted in his seat. He'd hoped this would be a dead end. *You never get one when you need one.*

He imagined Susan sitting where he was, Sasha's eyelids fluttering as she held his wife's hands. "Does Alan still love me?" he heard her ask. Yet he couldn't imagine Susan coming here alone. Not in this neighborhood. He pictured Anthony slipping a Slim Jim into his car window.

Run.

Not yet. He had to find out what Sasha knew.

"Was she with someone?" Jack asked.

"Yes." Sasha's eyelid twitched.

"Was it a woman?"

"Yes." Another twitch.

Susan must have come here with Emily. He couldn't imagine

Emily buying into all this mystic crap, but she couldn't help meddling in Susan's life—no matter where it led. Of course, that's assuming Sasha wasn't lying.

Susan would never come here. It's all BULL.

"Let me do a reading for you." Sasha pushed up her sleeves. "Maybe that will tell you what you need to know."

"Don't touch me." He stood so abruptly that his chair toppled over.

"Wait." Sasha picked up the chair. "I see letters. Sometimes there are lots of letters. Other times there's only one. With your wife, I only got the letter A."

Jack winced. Alan Dean. How he despised that fucking name. A sing-song chorus played inside his head: *Alan Dean, Susan's dream. Alan Dean, he be clean. Don't you mess with Alan Dean!*

Jack covered his ears. "Stop that!"

Sasha skipped rope to the beat of the song. Jack blinked, and the psychic was standing in front of him, looking at him as if

"You have voices in your head." Sasha reached into the red box on the table and removed a small bottle. It looked like something a genie ought to inhabit. "Take this." She closed her eyes as if it hurt to give it to him.

"What is it?"

Alan Dean, he's the man. He's the man who's got the plan!

"Oil you put on your chest." Sasha had a heart on her necklace. She rubbed it as it beat wildly. "It stops the voices."

Jack pictured himself rubbing the oil on his chest. Warmth spreads from his fingers down to his toes. *Maybe you're wrong about her.* His muscles relax, breathing slows. He's at peace. He looks down at his chest. There's a red spot, getting bigger, his veins bulge. There's a searing pain—a burning. He smells gasoline. His chest is on fire.

"Please take it, Mr. Logan. It will help you." Sasha put the genie bottle in his palm. It was hot.

"I don't want it." Jack threw the bottle at the wall. It shattered. The oil puddled on the floor, creeping towards him. He staggered backwards.

"That oil costs fifty dollars." Sasha put out her hand.

You have to get out of here. YOU HAVE TO.

Sasha pushed the button on the table. Jack lunged for the doorknob. Sasha grabbed his arm.

"Let go of me!" Jack yanked his arm from her grasp. Sasha stumbled.

The door opened. Anthony stood in the doorway, headphones around his neck. He opened his mouth to say something.

Jack thrust a fifty at him and ran.

CHAPTER 11

YOU NEED HELP.

Hire someone. He was desperate, and as Sean had reminded him, he always got the best.

Sean's right about that.

Jack was in his study. He sat back in his chair and tented his fingers. He wanted to be the one who found Alyson, but when he thought about what had happened with Alice Walker, he turned toward his computer and went to a national investigation firm's website. A little clicking disclosed that they didn't deal with missing persons. To hell with them. He went to another's site only to find that they didn't either.

That's an unexpected twist.

Jack wished he could get a recommendation from someone but he didn't have the first idea who to ask.

He opened the Yellow Pages. His hand was shaking. He found listings for such firms as: A-1 Investigations; Finders, Inc.; Premier Investigations; Sherlock, Inc.; and Worldwide Investigations.

Finders, Inc., intrigued him. But he decided to focus on someone who used their name.

A better chance they're legitimate.

Alan Adams's office was in Ridgewood, a good sign.

Wait—you can't work with anyone named Alan.

Jack dialed Ronald Born's number. A man answered with a confident "Hello" on the first ring.

"Is this Mr. Born?"

"Yes, speaking."

"My name is Jack Logan." He stood and started pacing. "I need to find a girl…I mean, someone named Alyson Walker."

"Hmmm, okay, a missing person, I'm sure we can help." He sounded like a college kid.

Jack said, "When were you born?"

"Huh?"

"How many missing person cases have you handled?"

"This would be my first."

"I need someone with experience," Jack said.

"I'll do a good job, and you don't pay me if I don't find them."

Hardly an enticement. But Born would likely be willing to work with Jack. The blind leading the blind?

"I have a law degree," he said, sounding even younger now. "And I'm into the latest technology."

"Why didn't you become a lawyer?"

"I couldn't stand being in an office."

Jack was intrigued but he couldn't get past the lack of experience.

You don't want to wind up with another Sean.

The next listing was for Bill Keene. Jack dialed his number. A recording said the number was no longer in service. He got the same result with Tony Lamont.

Jack began to sweat.

Maybe Born was your best bet after all.

The next ad was for a Reginald Murphy—the two-inch box

indicating he specialized in missing persons. Jack dialed his number.

Reggie Murphy sat at a large teak desk. He spread his long fingers, nails looking as if they'd been manicured. The private investigator was a big, muscular man, probably six-four and weighing a solid two-fifty. He had black curly hair and a dark handsome face.

"Someone recommend me to you, Mr. Logan?" Reggie's voice was deep, authoritative. Jack met his stare.

"I found you in the phone book."

Reggie propped a foot on an open drawer. He had on a crisp white shirt, a gray doubled-breasted suit, and a black tie with a silver stickpin. A taupe fedora hung on the hat rack behind him, looking over his shoulder as if covering his back.

"Before we get started you should know my retainer is five hundred." Reggie rubbed his thumbnail. "And I charge one-fifty an hour plus expenses." He looked Jack up and down. "I assume that's not a problem for you."

"It's not if you're good."

Reggie nodded. "I get results, but sometimes things take time. Not always, but sometimes." He leaned back in his leather chair and looked at Jack from half-closed eyes. "You a patient man, Mr. Logan?"

"I'm patient if I have to be." He uncrossed his legs then crossed them again. Reggie seemed to notice.

You need to stay calm.

"I'm good at what I do. I'm so good I get to choose who I work with"—Reggie stabbed his chest with his thumb—"and I only work with patient people. That's something we need to establish up front."

"Your ad said you're a former police detective?" Jack gripped the arms of his chair.

"For twenty-five years. I specialized in missing persons, retired last year. I was fed up with the bullshit, and now I don't have to take it anymore."

Jack pulled out his checkbook. His pen fell on the floor.

"I'll give you a check for five hundred now, and…" His fingers groped for the pen.

Reggie held up a hand. "First tell me what it is you want me to do." He cocked an eyebrow. "I might not want to do it."

Jack retrieved the pen and slipped it back into his pocket.

"I need you to help me find someone." He was pleased with this straightforward response.

"Help you?" Reggie leaned closer to him. "Are you looking for a partner or a missing person?" He pointed to himself. "I work alone."

"This is something I need a professional to do." Jack held up his hands. "I'm staying out of it." Reggie rubbed his lower lip and nodded.

Jack's heart raced.

You almost blew it.

"How long is this person missing?"

"Six months."

"The police haven't helped?"

"I haven't spoken to them."

"But you filed a missing person report?" The private investigator raised his brow.

"I assume someone has."

"What's this person's relation to you?" Reggie looked at him like he was nuts.

"She's no relation at all."

"How long have you known her?"

"I've never met her."

Reggie tilted his head. They held each other's gaze. Jack shrugged.

"And why do you want me to find her?"

"My wife died three months ago and this missing girl looks exactly like her."

Jack wondered what he would think if someone said that to him. He sat back in his seat, reversing the roles in his mind.

No. You're cool.

Jack relaxed.

"I'm sorry to hear about your loss." Reggie looked at his face intently. Jack felt like he was studying it. "But you're telling me the only reason you want to find this woman is because she looks like your wife?"

"She looks exactly like her. She could be her twin."

"But she's not?"

"That's one thing I'm sure of."

"This sounds nuts." The private investigator shook his head.

"I'll pay you two hundred an hour!"

"This isn't about money. This is about bullshit." Reggie took a big breath and blew it out. "And I can smell the bullshit on this one. Know what I do when I smell it? Go the other way. On the force, I couldn't walk away from bullshit." He grinned. "Now I can."

"My wife was pregnant when she died," Jack said. "We named the baby Alison. This missing girl has the same name."

Reggie looked up at the ceiling, then back at Jack. At least he hadn't rolled his eyes.

"She looks like your wife and has the same name as your unborn daughter?"

"Only the spelling is different."

Jack's cheek itched, but he wouldn't scratch it. He sat still and met Reggie's unwavering stare.

He thinks there's something wrong with you.

"What are you going to do after you find her?" Reggie asked.

"I'll know after I do."

"You want to marry her?" Reggie sat forward.

"Absolutely not," Jack said.

"How old is she?"

"Fifteen."

"She's a *teenager*?" Reggie pushed back his chair. "You kidding me?"

"No."

"Let me get this straight. You want me to find a teenage girl you've never met?"

"That's right."

"That's a complication, Mr. Logan." Reggie stood and started pacing. "That's a big complication."

"Call me Jack."

"I'll call you Jack, but it's still a complication."

"Why?"

What is the problem?

Reggie looked at him. Sighed. Shook his head.

"Some people may not like the idea of a stranger hiring a private investigator to find their missing kid. They might think you have an ulterior motive. They may not cooperate. That makes my job harder. That's unnecessary bullshit and you already know how I feel about that." He jerked his head toward the window behind him. "There are plenty of missing people out there. I'm passing on this one."

He knows you're nuts.

"I sense no one's looking for this girl," Jack said.

"You know that as a fact?"

He shook his head.

"See, I only deal with facts." Reggie pointed at him. "You'd do well to do the same, Jack."

"You've never had a hunch? A feeling that told you what you should do despite what logic said?"

"So you're in touch with your feelings?" Reggie asked.

"This is the exception."

Reggie sighed. "You got a picture of her?"

Jack reached into his inside jacket pocket and handed over the postcard.

"You said she's fifteen?" Reggie sat on the edge of his desk, leg dangling.

"It's got her date of birth."

"Fifteen-year-olds didn't look like this when I was growing up." Reggie flicked the postcard.

Jack flinched.

"You know anything about her?" Reggie held the postcard between his index fingers.

"Only what's on there." He pointed to it.

Reggie looked into the distance. Jack bit his lower lip as he listened to the seconds ticking by on Reggie's desk clock.

"Tell you what," he said. "Give me a check for five hundred and I'll do a preliminary investigation. I'll tell you what I come up with and if I want to continue on this case. That sound fair to you?"

"When can you start?" Jack pulled out his checkbook.

Reggie ran his tongue over his upper lip, pointed, and said, "Right after I get that check."

Chapter 12

Jack sat at his kitchen table. Sun poured into the room from the picture window above the white porcelain sink. He stared out the window until the sunlight hurt his eyes.

A dull ache throbbed at his temples—a pain he hoped to remedy with a solid dose of caffeine. The coffeemaker gurgled as a rich brown liquid dripped into the glass pot. The scent of coffee drifting toward his nose was wonderful.

Susan never drank coffee, but she loved the smell of it. She said so when he made it every morning. He could still hear the joy in her voice, still hear the way she never failed to emphasize the word "love."

The coffeemaker burped.

He looked up.

The glass pot was full—his morning medicine freshly brewed. The scent of the coffee found him again. So did Susan's voice. But this time it was telling Alan how much she loved him. *Always have, always will.*

Jack rose from the table and poured the coffee into a blue

mug with the word HIS in big black letters across the front of it. In the oak cabinet above his head was a pink mug with the word HERS on it. Susan had bought the mugs on their last trip to Bermuda. That was where she'd emerged from the bathroom with a blue stick saying she was pregnant with Alison.

They had his and hers bathrobes. His and hers towels. Susan had bought these things, fooled him into believing her heart wasn't with someone else during the time they were together.

He looked around the kitchen.

Memories are everywhere.

There were too many memories and they were all too easy to find—pieces of his past gnawing at his brain everywhere he looked.

He brought the mug to his lips. The coffee slid down his throat and warmed him. He drank it black, hoping for a caffeine rush. He got a gentle buzz instead—one that let in a ray of optimism. Had Susan loved him as much as she loved Alan? Was she torn between two loves?

The phone rang.

He picked up on the third ring.

"We're still on for today?" It was Emily.

People needing money are relentless.

"Can you come by at noon?" Ten, twelve, and two—his appointments were always at one of these times if he had a choice in the matter.

"I have a yoga class at twelve."

"You take yoga?"

Emily was slender and claimed she never worked at it. He believed her.

"It's Bikram Yoga. The classes are in a room that's a hundred and five degrees. It cleanses your body, clears your mind, and it might even be good for your soul."

"I didn't think you liked to sweat."

"There are times I choose to."

"Did Susan ever go with you?"

You need to be more subtle.

"I gave her a flyer. She gave me one of her 'someday maybe' answers."

Was Emily leading him somewhere, or just leading him on? Could he trust her? He needed to find that out.

"Would you like to stay for lunch?" He wiped his upper lip. The coffee and the conversation conspired to make him sweat.

"What were you thinking?" She sounded surprised.

"I can grill a couple of steaks."

"I can't eat steak after yoga. It's too much of a contradiction too soon." He heard what sounded like cigarette smoke against her mouthpiece. "Besides, I'm the one borrowing money. I should take you out to lunch."

She should tell you why she needs the money.

"I can be at your house at two. You can give me the check and then we'll go out to eat. My treat…no if, ands, or buts about it."

"Let's stay here. I'll make my Caesar salad and I'll get some baguettes. You like cheese?"

"Gouda, brie, and alpine lace are my favorites."

"Good." He grabbed a pen, found a piece of paper, and started a list. "We'll do vegetarian—a lunch that'll make the Maharishi proud."

He wouldn't give her fifty thousand without knowing why she wanted it. He was still hoping she'd tell him. But if he had to ask, he'd rather do it in his house.

"Sure you wouldn't rather go out, Jack?"

"I'm positive."

"Then I'll see you at two."

He heard a click. He held the handset in his lap as he stared at the wall.

The phone rang. It was Reggie.

"I've got some information. You home for a while?"

"Yes." Jack cleared his throat, wishing he had more notice

but knowing he couldn't ask for it. It was Friday. He'd hired the private investigator yesterday. After Reggie's dissertation on patience, Jack hadn't expected to hear from him this week.

"I'm not far from you." It sounded like Reggie was driving. Jack thought he could hear 'Living for the City' in the background. A horn beeped. "Be there in ten minutes, maybe less."

"I'll see you then."

Jack put the phone back in its base and ran up the stairs. He went into the bathroom. He turned on the water and studied the mirror. He blinked. Susan was coming towards him.

His wife liked to wrap her arms around him while he was at the bathroom sink, often when his face was dripping with soap or his mouth filled with toothpaste. He was always focused on what he was doing at the time and found it hard to respond.

You wasted those moments with her.

He reached for her image.

The doorbell rang.

He checked over his shoulder. When he turned back to the mirror, Susan was gone. He shut off the water and buttoned his shirt going down the stairs.

The bell rang again.

Jack opened the front door.

Reggie was wearing a black double-breasted suit that fit him perfectly. A white silk handkerchief was tucked in his breast pocket. His shirt was light blue with a white collar. His red tie had a diamond stickpin. The man could dress.

Reggie nodded, stepped past him, and stood in the hallway.

"You want coffee?" Jack needed another cup, having not finished his first.

"Just ate breakfast," Reggie patted his stomach and shoved his head toward the living room. "In there's fine with me."

Jack followed Reggie and turned on the track lighting, sliding the dimmer to bright.

The room was huge. A fireplace lay opposite the entrance, a bar in the left corner. On the right, a white leather couch, loveseat, and chair surrounded a glass coffee table.

"Nice place you got here." Reggie said, looking around, his hands on his hips.

"Thanks." Jack inhaled. Reggie had on cologne—a complex scent.

The big man sat on the chair and stretched out his legs.

"Mind if I ask what you do for a living?"

"I was a stock trader." Jack sat on the couch, the private investigator on his left.

"Was?" Reggie creased his forehead. "You retired?"

"I quit trading after my wife died. Don't know if I'll ever do it again."

"What you are doing now?"

"I'm trying to find Alyson Walker." He stared at the bar. "Sure you don't want something to drink?"

"I'm fine for now." Reggie examined his nails. He did that a lot. "This place is immaculate. Who's your cleaning lady? I'd like to hire her."

We should be talking about Alyson.

"I clean myself." Jack tightened his jaw.

Reggie nodded as if he'd expected that answer.

"What?" Jack asked.

"Nothing," Reggie said with a shrug.

"Come on, Reggie, be straight with me."

"That's what you really want?"

"It is if we're going to do business together." Jack knew Reggie would like that answer.

"You're right." Reggie wiggled his index finger. "No bullshit between us." The PI stared at the wall behind Jack.

"So?" Jack drummed the table. "Let's hear it."

"I know you're going through a tough time. But I sense you're not heading in the best direction."

You've got to watch yourself with him.

"What makes you think that?" Jack asked as calmly as he could.

"People are my job. It doesn't take me long to figure them out, and I'm usually right about them once I do."

"I'm hiring you to find Alyson, not to analyze me." He flicked a piece of lint from his pants, breaking from the private investigator's gaze. Staring was something else Reggie did a lot.

"We agreed, Jack. No bullshit between us." Reggie put his hands behind his head and leaned back. "I'm just keeping to that."

"And now that you have, can we get to Alyson?"

"I can't imagine what you must be feeling, but there comes a time when you've just got to say 'screw you, world' and push past it all. It's the only way to survive."

Their eyes were fixed on each other.

"What do you think?" Reggie pulled out a small, top-bound spiral notebook from his inside jacket pocket and flipped past the first couple of pages.

"I think we should get back to Alyson."

"Okay, Jack." Reggie held up his hands—the pad in one, a pen in the other. He appeared to contemplate something, then dismiss it. "I spoke to the detective investigating Alyson's disappearance. She's someone I used to work with."

The postcard was real. Jack's heart beat faster.

"Alyson's mother was Mary Walker," Reggie said.

"Was?"

"She died six months ago. It wasn't long after the funeral when Alyson went missing. The police believe she took some of the money her mother left her and ran away."

"What about her father?"

"That's where it gets interesting." Reggie put the notebook

on the coffee table. "Mary Walker got divorced eight years ago, when Alyson was seven. She'd been married to John Walker, the independent film producer. Ever hear of him?"

"No."

"I've seen two of John Walker's movies," Reggie said. "He's into edgy stuff. There's violence and sex, but it's all subtle and very real." He raised his eyebrows. "The guy's good."

Jack's and Susan's tastes in movies didn't agree. So he devoured stock market data and read psychological suspense novels, intending to write one someday. Susan perused catalogues and did all the exercises in self-help books.

"Could Alyson be with him?" Jack asked.

"John Walker claims he hasn't seen or talked to Alyson since the divorce. So far, the police believe him."

"But she's his daughter."

"Mary adopted Alyson before she met John." Reggie picked up the notebook and checked something. "He said the only thing he gave Alyson was her last name."

Jack nodded slowly. Now Alyson was more than just a girl in a photograph with an intriguing name. Now he had some facts about her. He sensed there was pain in her life and he had a feel for its nature. She probably didn't trust a lot of people. She was probably lonely.

Two things you can relate to.

"So who reported her missing?" Jack was impressed with the information Reggie had gathered so far.

HE HAS TO TAKE THIS CASE!

"Doris Chance. She was a neighbor—her son, Nolan, is Alyson's friend. Nolan said Alyson had talked about running away after the funeral. She didn't want to wind up in a foster home."

"So they're ruling out abduction?"

"Pretty much," Reggie said, "though you can never be sure."

Offer him two-fifty an hour.

"Mary had no relatives who could take care of Alyson?"

"No, and now the Chances have moved. I don't have their new address yet." Reggie stretched. "I've got someone working on that. I'll have it soon."

He's confident.

"So you're taking the case?"

"Jack, remember when I told you I work alone?" Reggie looked at his shoes. They were wing-tipped and shined like they'd just been polished.

He's clean and neat. He's organized. He's your man.

"We both know that's not happening if I take this case," Reggie said, standing up.

Jack rose and stood in front of him.

Offer him more money, as much as it takes. Don't lose him.

"You think I'm going to butt in?" Jack looked up at Reggie. He was at least three inches taller.

"I think you're the kind of person who needs to be directly involved."

"Are you a PI or a psychiatrist?" Jack said.

"You know the answer to that."

"I think it'd be a good thing if I'm involved," Jack said.

"Not if we start tripping over each other. Jack, this is serious stuff."

"Come on, Reggie, we're talking about a missing girl. How dangerous can it be?"

"Enough that it requires a clear head."

"You're not giving me much credit."

"Let me say it this way," Reggie said. "Emotions distort judgment."

"I'll keep mine in check."

"Make sure it's the emotions and not the judgment."

"So you're taking the case?" Jack felt a surge of optimism.

Reggie put up a hand. "Not so fast."

He's dragging this scene out.

"Reggie, I'll let you know what I'm doing before I do it. We can work this out. We just need to communicate."

You? Communicate?

"Listen, I've got to meet another client." Reggie tapped his watch. "You'll be here at five?"

Jack took a breath. Emily was coming at two.

You'll get rid of her by four-thirty.

"That'll work." He smiled as he imagined pushing Emily out the door.

Reggie looked at him. "I want to help you, Jack, but we need to establish some ground rules and we need to stick to them."

"I'll do whatever it takes. I just want you on this case."

"I'm serious about sticking to them."

"You can trust me, Reggie. Have I given you a reason to think otherwise?" Jack crossed his fingers behind his back.

Reggie gave him a long look. "See you at five," he said.

Jack went down the hall towards the kitchen, needing more coffee. His mind worked through the information Reggie had given him, taking it apart and putting it back together again, knowing some of it contained clues he needed.

You better not regret not offering him more money.

He heard a knock on the door.

The sun clock on the wall to his left said it was nine-forty.

There was only one person it could be.

Chapter 13

Jack opened the front door. Marjorie had on black pants and a red blouse.

"Any chance a girl can get a cup of coffee here?" she said.

He waved her in.

They went down the wide hallway that led to the kitchen. Abstract sculptures were on one side, surreal paintings on the other. Susan had bought all of them. Mementos from places they'd visited together.

Was she wishing she'd been there with Alan Dean?

With that thought, he stopped short.

Marjorie ran into him. He felt her hands on his back.

She went to the sink and started rinsing out the coffeepot. Her movements were focused and efficient, reminding him of Susan's.

"Even here I have to do this for you." She shook her head and dried her hands. "So, how are you doing?"

He rubbed his jaw. "I'll let you know next week."

Marjorie seemed to study him as she leaned against the counter.

"I'm sorry about coming over like this. But I wanted to talk to you in person and I couldn't wait any longer."

"It's no problem." He crossed his arms. It still hurt that she'd told Sean she was leaving before she told him. But he couldn't be angry at her.

"Sean told you I resigned?" Marjorie grabbed the coffeepot and turned on the cold water.

"Yes." His heart beat faster. "Is it because of him?" Jack imagined his hands around Sean's neck, choking him, his partner's eyes bulging, his mouth bloody.

"Not at all. It's something I've wanted to do for a while." She opened one cabinet door after another. "Now the time is right." Her back was to him. She had broad shoulders and a narrow waist.

Jack reached around her and handed her the coffee canister.

"Thanks." There was a beat. "Are you okay with the month's notice?"

Jack nodded, words stuck in his throat.

"That'll give you and Sean enough time to find my replacement."

"No one can replace you."

"Jack."

"I'll give you a raise." He liked knowing Marjorie was there to keep an eye on Sean now that he wasn't.

What the hell, keep trying to solve problems with money.

"This isn't about money," Marjorie said. "We both know you already pay me more than I'd make anywhere else." That was supposed to lock her up for life—a small price to pay that hadn't paid off.

Dust motes swirled in the air. Bars of sunlight fell across the kitchen counter. A fly buzzed Jack's ear. He tried to grab it and missed. The fly landed on the center island. Jack lunged for it and knocked over a bowl of fake fruit. He watched it fall to the floor as the fly escaped. Jack picked up the bowl and put the fruit back in. One piece at a time.

It has to be EXACTLY the way Susan had it.

"Is there a problem?" Marjorie asked.

"Were the pears on top or on the bottom? And the grapes, where were they?"

"It's not important."

Jack continued to arrange the fruit. But it didn't seem right.

"Jack, forget about the fruit. Talk to me." Marjorie picked up an apple.

"I want everything back the way it was."

"You can't."

"Don't say that!" He snatched the apple out of her hand, scratching her finger.

"That hurt." Marjorie stepped back.

You're scaring her.

"I'm sorry," he said. "Are you okay?"

"I'm fine." Marjorie sucked the scrape on her finger.

Jack cleared his throat.

"What will you do?" he said. "You're not one to sit around the house watching daytime TV."

"Steve has his twenty-five years and is finally ready to retire." Her husband was a homicide detective who seemed destined to die on the job, one way or another. He was finally getting smart before he did. "We're going to buy a Winnebago, drive cross country, and try to save our marriage."

She wasn't just quitting. She was leaving.

You're losing her, too.

He gripped the center island as if it were the last of his sanity.

"Jack, what's wrong?"

He shook his head.

She held his arms. "I know…this is the last thing you needed."

"It's not just that." He looked around. "It's…it's everything."

The room was spinning. He saw Alyson being sucked into the vortex of a tornado. He reached for her and yelled, "Alyson!"

"You keep thinking about your daughter." Marjorie had sympathetic eyes.

"It's not her."

"It's not?"

The fly buzzed his ear again. It would die eventually, probably where he'd never find it—death everywhere. He shivered.

"Let's sit for a minute." Marjorie took his hand.

He pulled it back. "I need to get that damn fly. You see it?"

"Jack, this isn't good." She sighed. "You really should see someone. I know a—"

"What, a shrink? That's your answer?"

"It might help." She bit her lower lip.

"Lying on a couch and talking about my problems won't cure me." His voice boomed. "Doing something might."

"You know I know you, and you know I care." Marjorie pulled in a breath. "Jack, this path you're on, looking for this girl?" *Sean the blabbermouth.* "I don't think it's going to lead you to a good place. Don't take it."

"I have to."

It's your only way out.

Marjorie turned and spooned coffee into a filter.

"As for my leaving—I'm sorry, Jack, but I can't wait any longer. This is the only chance Steve and I have left."

"Steve's a lucky bastard." He put a hand on her shoulder. "You've done everything I've ever asked and so much more. Do what you need to."

You're not as brave as you sound.

A tear slipped down Marjorie's cheek. She wiped it with her finger. She tried to smile but couldn't quite manage it.

"You can always call me. Whenever you need to talk, I'll always be there to listen."

He knew she meant it, but he also knew time and distance would eventually change things.

Jack heard laughter and looked out the window. A little boy was chasing a girl in the yard next door. The boy fell, got up, and ran after the girl again.

"I'm going to miss you." He reached for her.

She stepped closer and kissed his cheek.

"I love you, Jack Logan." She'd never told him that before.

"Love you too." He held her tight. There it was. The fly was by the window, flicking the pane. Taunting him.

"Please take care of yourself," Marjorie said. "I'm worried about you."

"Don't be." He looked at her. "I just need time to get my head right."

What you need is to kill that fly.

They shared a cup of coffee with no conversation he could remember. Then he watched Marjorie walk down the stone path that led away from his house. She waved, hesitated, got in her car and drove off.

Jack went back inside and closed the door. He bent over. His arms wrapped his stomach as emptiness filled him.

He'd just lost the only person he trusted now that Susan was gone.

Finding Alyson Walker is all you have left.

Chapter 14

IT WAS NOON. Emily would be there in two hours. Jack was in the upstairs bathroom mopping the floor. Once he finished, the entire house would be—

The phone rang.

He stepped back and his foot hit the bucket behind him, spilling dirty water on the white tile floor.

Now you'll have to wash it again.

Jack went into his bedroom, muttering obscenities. He checked the phone's Caller ID and winced.

You're NOT answering.

"Jack…this is Sean. If you're there please pick up." His partner's voice was loud and clear.

"I wish I wasn't," Jack shouted at the answering machine.

"Listen…I feel bad about what happened at breakfast the other day."

"I don't." Jack hit his head with the heel of his hand.

"Jack, I really need your help. I can't do this by myself any longer….Things are starting to get out of control."

"Starting to?" Jack laughed and spread his arms. "Welcome to the club."

"I got a margin call this morning—I need to figure out what to sell. Please call me."

Jack's mind instinctively began ticking off steps to take, then it froze.

You can't go back there.

"I know. It was a stupid mistake….Today we lost two more clients."

Jack felt blood rush to his face. "Use your guilt to help you!" His finger hovered over the answering machine's stop button. He wished pushing it was all it would take to banish his partner to oblivion.

"Please, call as soon as you can." It sounded like Sean was taking a sip of something.

"Are you drunk?"

"You have my number," Sean said.

"I wish I didn't."

Jack sat at the head of his oak dining room table. It could seat a dozen but was set for two. Afternoon sunlight bled through the vertical blinds on the sliding glass doors behind him. Outside, a deck ran the width of his house.

Emily was seated on his right, wearing a short, white summer dress. Her red hair was pinned up behind her head, her sandals on the floor next to her bare feet.

They'd just finished lunch. Jack pushed off the arms of his chair.

"Don't go anywhere. I'll be right back." He went upstairs to get the fifty-thousand-dollar check he'd already made out to Emily White.

He slid it off his bedroom dresser and looked at it. He'd thought and thought about what he should write in the memo line: *Emily Loan* or *No Friggin Idea* or a series of question marks? He finally left it blank.

First time you've ever done that.

He folded the check in half and slipped it into in his shirt pocket.

He had to admit, lunch with Emily wasn't as uncomfortable as he thought it would be. The conversation flowed easily between them, easier than it ever had before.

She even made him laugh with a story about a couple with no relatives who wanted to buy a huge house. He couldn't recall the last time he'd laughed. It sounded like business was good for Susan's half-sister, despite the weakness in the real estate market.

Then why does she need the damn money?

He heard a chair move.

It's time you found that out.

He headed back downstairs.

Emily was picking up plates and silverware in the dining room. He took what she had in her hands, put everything in the sink, and rolled up his sleeves. He only used the dishwasher when he had a full load—which was almost never.

Emily dried what he washed, making room in the dish drainer for what he'd put in next. They worked together in a comfortable silence, efficiently and effectively, as if they'd done this many times before. It reminded him of yesterday, when he was in the kitchen with Marjorie. When he realized just how good it was not to be alone.

Washing dishes—one of the few things that didn't elicit memories of his wife. He and Susan ate out most nights and always used the dishwasher when they didn't.

After he and Emily finished up in the kitchen, they went into the living room and sat across from one another on the white leather couch Susan loved.

Emily, still barefoot, tucked her feet under her. Her legs were slender, calves taut. She removed two pins from her hair and shook it until it fell over her shoulders and down her back.

"Would you like a martini now?" He had offered to make her one when she arrived, but she wanted to eat first.

"Just don't make it dirty." She sat against the corner of the couch. "It's still too soon after yoga for that."

"One clean vodka martini coming up," he said as he rose, relieved he didn't have to make something dirty.

"Are you joining me?" Emily hugged a leather pillow.

"It's too early for me." He tapped his watch. It was just after three.

"You need to loosen up, Jack."

"I will when I'm ready." He balled his hands, anger bubbling inside him.

They stared at each other like two gunslingers waiting to see who'd make the first move—their first uncomfortable moment that afternoon.

"Sure," Emily said after a beat.

Jack turned and went behind the wet bar.

"You have a preference on vodka?" He held up a bottle in each hand like a fisherman showing off his catch.

"Surprise me," Emily said to the ceiling, her back to him. "I'm sure you have an excellent selection."

"Thought you didn't like surprises?" He thumped the bottles down on top of the bar and checked to see which had the higher proof. Both were eighty.

"I like surprises if I can choose when they happen." Emily stretched, and the track lighting caught gold highlights in her hair.

"You're anal." He set a double shot glass down on top of the bar.

"We have that in common." Emily looked at him from over her shoulder.

"Being anal is a pain in the ass." He took the cover off the ice bucket. The silver cocktail shaker clanged as he dropped six cubes in it.

He poured the second double shot of Grey Goose into the cocktail shaker, shook it over one shoulder and then the other. He filled a large martini glass, dropped in three olives skewered by a red plastic sword, and took small steps as he brought the drink to Emily. He handed her the glass, slipping a coaster off the stack of them on the coffee table.

"I might've made it a little strong."

Emily took a sip and jerked her head back as if she'd taken a punch.

"A *little?*" She chewed an olive and looked at him. "Are you trying to get me drunk?"

He reached for her glass. "Let me make you another."

"It's fine." She slapped his hand away. "Just make the next one weaker."

"I will, but it still won't be dirty." He sat on the couch next to her, pulled the check from his shirt pocket, and handed it to her. "As promised."

"Thank you." Emily unfolded the check and looked at it.

You should've put something on the memo line.

His nose found the delicate scent of her perfume.

"You know, it was hard for me to ask you for this money." She waved the check like a flag. "I'm used to dealing with challenges on my own."

"It's no problem."

"Is it no problem because you have bunches of money?" she asked.

"No, it's because…" He studied the white carpeting. It had been delivered on a rainy day in the spring of 2005. After the installers left, Susan put down a blanket next to the fireplace and they made love.

"It's because you feel guilty." Emily's words felt like a slap.

Tension filled the room. He moved his eyes from side to side. She liked to toy with him, see how he reacted.

"That one hurt." He rubbed the side of face,

"I'm sorry." Her hand found his arm. "Sometimes I go too far."

He shrugged. "I deserve it."

"No, you don't."

"You really believe that?" He cocked an eyebrow.

"Wouldn't have said it if I didn't." She put her hand on his shoulder. "And now I'll let you in on a little secret."

His mind darted for possibilities. Thoughts bounced off the walls of his imagination. He ducked.

"I don't need this money," she whispered, alcohol on her breath. She tore the check into fourths and dropped it in his hand. Then she downed the last of her drink.

"What? You were testing me?" Anger hit his chest.

"I wanted to know if you'd lend it to me. I wanted to know if you trusted me." She looked down and curled her painted toes into the deep pile carpet.

"And just when I'm starting to trust you, you give me a reason not to." He rose from the couch and stood above her. "You're destructive, Emily."

"Loneliness does that to you." She looked up at him. "We know that."

"What, so you no longer blame me for what happened to Susan?" He turned the pieces of the check into a ball and dropped it on the coffee table. They watched it roll toward the coaster.

"Face it, Jack, you screwed up." Emily put her heels on the coffee table. "Everyone does once in a while, even Susan. You were just unlucky enough to do it at the worst possible time."

He was about to explode. But he needed to stay focused. He needed the truth.

He sat back down.

"At Daniela's you said Susan wasn't as perfect as people believed." He was on the edge of his seat. "What did you mean by that?"

Emily sighed. "For that, I'll need another drink." She handed him her empty glass.

He wanted Emily to tell him something about Susan he already knew, or at least something that wouldn't surprise him. *You know it won't be either.*

Emily moved to the edge of the bar, her flat stomach pressed against the thick black cushion that wrapped its perimeter. She watched as he poured one double shot into the shaker.

"There was something Susan wanted to tell you but never got the chance," Emily said.

He made the drink and filled a fresh glass, trying to keep his hand steady. He dropped in three more olives and slid the martini over to her.

Emily sat on the middle stool and stabbed the top of the bar with her elbows. She looked like she could use a cigarette.

"Susan got pregnant when she was nineteen," she said. "Alan Dean was the father."

Their eyes locked.

He held the sides of the bar. *Susan was an unwed mother?* He couldn't conceive of that.

"She found out she was pregnant after Alan left her," Emily said. "She had a girl and gave her away. Alan still doesn't know."

He shook his head violently. "Susan would've told me this."

"It happened." Emily lowered her eyes. "I know it for a fact."

"No. She never told me." He stared into the distance. In the hall was a painting in all dark colors—a man alone, rowing against a raging ocean.

He knew Susan had secrets. When she was alive he believed he knew all the secrets that mattered—the ones that made her who she was.

Wrong!

"She never told anyone." Emily stirred her drink.

"I'm not anyone." He stepped out from behind the bar. "I was her husband. I loved her. I'd have accepted anything about her." He started pacing. "She had to have known that."

"She saw it as a black mark on her life." Emily blocked his path. "You know how Susan felt about anything black." She tried to smile, didn't make it.

"Why did you know?" He crossed his arms.

"Only because she hid out at my apartment until after she had the baby," Emily said.

"What happened to her child?" He imagined Susan giving birth. He heard a newborn cry.

"She gave her to a woman who worked for an adoption agency. Susan knew she'd give the baby a good home and knew everything would happen quickly and discreetly. It was the only good thing in a bad situation."

He headed toward the kitchen. His mouth tasted bitter. He wanted to spit. From the corner of his eye he saw Emily pick up her drink and follow him.

He stood by the kitchen sink. He downed a glass of water and then another.

"She always missed her daughter, Jack. But when she got pregnant again, she missed her even more." Emily's voice was soft. "Susan thought it would pass. It didn't."

More secrets, more his wife didn't tell him.

When does it end?

Jack wanted to destroy something. He jammed his hands deep into his pockets.

"So only you knew how she felt when she got pregnant again?" His wife, lover, and friend couldn't tell him what she felt.

That was your fault, too.

"She only confided in me because I already knew about her first child."

"That doesn't make me feel better."

"She tried getting past it," Emily said with her back to him. "She wrote letters to her daughter, apologizing. She even thought naming your baby Alison would help. Nothing did."

"Why wouldn't she tell me what she was going through?" He grabbed her bicep and turned her towards him, rocking her drink. "What the hell am I missing?"

"She wanted it behind her, Jack." Emily downed the last of her martini and put the empty glass in the sink. She wiped her lips with her index finger.

"It's like I didn't know her."

"There were things Susan kept to herself." She poked him. "You two had that in common."

"You said she was going to tell me?"

"After your anniversary."

That was two days after Susan died. They had reservations at The Soul Creek Inn and Spa. It was to be their last vacation before Alison was born.

"Why are you telling me this now?"

"Susan realized she had to know how her daughter was doing. She wanted you to help her."

"She wanted to meet her?"

"Not necessarily, just make sure she was loved and happy."

"You said Susan knew the woman who adopted her would give her a good home."

"She had to make sure. It was fifteen years ago—stuff happens, Jack. Susan hoped knowing her daughter had a good life would enable her to move on."

"Why would Susan think naming our baby Alison would help?"

"The woman who adopted Susan's child wanted to name her Susan. Susan asked her to name the baby Alyson—the one thing she did for Alan."

"She named her what?" he yelled.

"Alyson." Emily looked confused.

His body shook. He should've seen it sooner.

You were blinded by guilt and pain.

"You okay?" Emily stepped towards him.

"You said she wrote letters to Alyson?"

"She never mailed them, but yeah."

Susan's letter was to Alyson. He'd betrayed his wife by doubting her love for him. He closed his eyes and felt them burn.

"Alyson is missing." He sat at the kitchen table and looked up at the blank television screen, recalling the image of the newscaster and the picture over her shoulder.

"What are you talking about?" Emily asked.

"Susan's daughter, she's missing."

"What do you mean? You didn't know she existed until two minutes ago."

"Wait here." He shot up the stairs.

Now the stakes were higher. He couldn't help Susan, but he could help her daughter. His world wasn't what he thought it was, but at least it was starting to make sense.

"Wow!" Emily dropped Alyson's postcard on the kitchen table and pointed to it. "What did you think when you got that?"

"I thought it wasn't real." He remembered the picture on the milk carton that defied reality. "I thought I was losing my mind. But I knew I had to find her."

"I need a cigarette." Emily opened her pocketbook and pulled out a pack.

They stepped out onto the deck. The sun was bright, the air warm and muggy. Emily leaned against the deck's white railing, a rose-of-Sharon behind her.

"That's what you've been doing these past months, looking for Alyson?" Emily lit a cigarette.

"I only started last week."

"What were you doing before that?" She sucked in a lungful of smoke.

"Going insane," Jack said.

"I bet," she said. "What do you know about Alyson?"

He told her about Mary Walker dying, the Chances, Nolan Chance's telling the police Alyson had planned to run away after her mother's funeral. He didn't mention Sasha or Susan's letter.

"So Reggie thinks she's a runaway?" Emily said.

"She didn't want to wind up in a foster home."

"What are you going to do?" Emily's perspiration mingled with her cigarette smoke and perfume, a musky scent.

"I'm going to find her, tell her what I know, and help her do whatever she wants to do."

"What do you think that could be?"

"I have no idea."

"She may want to find Alan." Emily palmed his shoulder. "He's the only parent she has left. Susan wouldn't want Alyson to wind up with him."

"He's her father. It's probably what's best." Jack wasn't so sure, but it sounded like the right thing to say.

"Alan Dean is a bastard. You need to find him, you'll see for yourself."

"Find Alan Dean?"

"Trust me, woman's intuition, whatever. It's the right thing to do."

"You make it sound easy." He spread his arms. "You make it sound like I can just go around FINDING people."

You can't find yourself.

"It's not as difficult as you think." She looked at him. "I know where he is."

CHAPTER 15

REGGIE SHOWED UP AT FIVE SHARP. He and Jack headed for the living room and sat in the same spots as the day before: Jack on the couch, Reggie to his left in the thick chair. The private investigator looked more serious today.

"Can I get you something to drink?" Jack asked.

"Ice water," Reggie said.

It was another hot day, but Reggie still wore a suit and tie. It seemed like that was all he wore. Jack had yet to see the man sweat.

Jack was halfway down the hallway to the kitchen when the lights went out. He stopped. The lights came back on. Jack sighed, relieved. Then they went out again. This time they stayed out.

Susan had wanted him to buy a generator before Alison was born—one that came on automatically if they lost power. He'd researched the best one to buy and narrowed it down to two choices. That was just before the accident. He hadn't thought about the generator since.

Crap.

He poked his head into the living room and told Reggie he'd check things out.

Jack opened the front door and saw his neighbor across the street pulling into his driveway. His garage door rose—no power problem there. Lights were on in the house next door.

He went into the study. Its bay window let in plenty of light. He called the electric company from his cell phone. There were no reported outages in the area.

Jack went back into the living room. Reggie was sitting with his arms draped over his knees like a basketball player anxious to get into the game.

"It's only my house," Jack said.

"You have a flashlight?"

"I'll be right back."

The air inside the house was still. At least it was cool. It wouldn't be for much longer with no air conditioning.

Jack got the flashlight and found Reggie in the hallway. The PI had taken off his jacket, loosened his tie, and unbuttoned the top buttons on his shirt. He wore spread collars.

"Circuit box down here?" Reggie already had his hand on the knob of the door that led to the basement.

Where was the circuit box?

Jack looked around. The walls were moving towards him, and they were blue, not white. The sun clock was gone. So were the abstract paintings and sculptures.

Where'd they go?

He was back in his parent's house. His hands were tiny and he was wearing his blue pajamas with feet. Everything was blue, including him. He'd just cut the cord on his electric scissors. Sliced it clean in two. Gotten a good shock. "You need to be more RESPONSIBLE," his father told him. Words of reprimand. Words that—

"Stop," Jack said.

"Jack," Reggie said, "where's the circuit box?"

"Huh?"

"You okay?"

"Sure."

Reggie moved closer. "You look like you've seen a ghost."

"I have."

"What are you talking about?"

"Forget it." The walls were white and back where they should be. So were the pictures and sculptures. "It's in the basement. The circuit box is in the basement."

Jack wasn't mechanically inclined. He knew who to call for whatever he needed done. He could have an electrician at the house within an hour, but he sensed he should let Reggie help out.

"Lead the way." Reggie opened the basement door and stepped back.

Jack moved past him and flipped the light switch at the top of the stairs.

Duh. No electricity.

He shined the flashlight ahead and went downstairs, Reggie right behind him.

The basement was finished, paneled in oak. Sunlight entered from a ground-level window. Beneath it was a mirror, with a weight bench and a rack of dumbbells to one side. A treadmill faced the television on the opposite wall. Susan had wanted to replace it with a wide-screen high-def LCD. Jack had been researching those, too.

Susan ran on the treadmill three days a week, unless it was sunny and the temperature outside was above sixty-five degrees. Then she'd do four laps around the neighborhood dressed all in white—sneakers, socks, shorts, and cut-off tee shirt. Sometimes he sat on the front porch and waited for her to pass by.

You didn't do it enough.

Reggie's heels clicked on the parquet floor as Jack led him to the circuit panel in an unfinished alcove off the main room. The scent of burning plastic lingered in the air.

"You smell that?" Jack asked.

"Yeah." An emergency light shone on the circuit panel, illuminating faint wisps of rising smoke. Reggie took the flashlight from Jack, opened the panel door, and threw light on the black rocker switches inside. Some were in the off position.

"You have a generator?"

"Not yet." Jack fiddled with the cap of the hand sanitizer in his pocket. "But I had the transfer switch installed for when I decide on one."

Reggie shined the flashlight on the first circuit panel.

"The smell and smoke are definitely coming from here." He opened the door on the circuit panel, pulled down the handle marked MAIN, and grinned.

"Now I can't get fried."

"You know anything about electricity, Reggie?"

Reggie handed the flashlight back to Jack. It was warm. Jack shivered. His hands felt dirty.

"My father was an electrician. Had his own business." Reggie sighed. "Worked it until the day he died. I used to help him while I was going to college."

Jack wanted to tell Reggie he'd call the electrician. He wanted them to get back to looking for Alyson. But he knew he had to let this play out. Frustration brewed inside him as his finger clicked the cap on the hand sanitizer. Open and shut, faster and faster. Open and shut. Open and shut. Open—

"You have any tools?" Reggie asked.

Jack had plenty. A housewarming present from Susan's father, who firmly believed there were certain things a man should have, and a good set of tools was one of them. They were under the basement steps, right where Jack had put them the day he got them.

"Nice," Reggie said after opening the large red metal box and sorting through its contents. He pulled out a long screwdriver and a set of Allen wrenches.

They went back to the alcove.

Reggie started to remove the screws that held the front of the circuit panel in place.

Jack held the flashlight and imagined a giant clock, its hands spinning out of control. Alyson was out there. Susan's daughter. They were losing time. He felt powerless. He reached in his pocket and squeezed the sanitizer bottle.

SHIT!

The cold liquid squirted inside his pocket—he'd left the cap off. His body shook. He felt his face redden.

How could you be so stupid?

In high school Sissy Peters had rubbed against his crotch while they were kissing. He let go of his feelings. He erupted—thick and slimy, squirting, it showed on his pants.... Embarrassment didn't come close to describing how he felt. Humiliation wasn't—

"Jack...take this." Reggie handed him the last screw, then pulled off the circuit box cover and leaned it against the wall.

"You don't have to do this, Reggie." Jack stared at the wires now exposed, his heart racing. He'd had enough of this. Reggie had to know they were wasting precious time.

"We've got more important things to deal with," he said.

"Almost done, Jack." Reggie took a large Allen wrench and tightened three bolts. "Now let's see. . . ." He pushed up the main circuit.

The lights came back on.

After a minute, there was no smoke and no smell.

Reggie smiled and looked up. "Thanks, Dad."

"What was wrong?" Jack turned to conceal the stain on his pants.

"Two bolts on the main feed were loose." Reggie put the

Allen wrench back in the plastic pouch and headed toward the stairs. Jack followed him.

"Alyson looks like my wife for a reason." Jack watched Reggie put the tools away.

"Which is?" Reggie squatted over the red chest.

"She's Susan's daughter."

"How'd you find that out?"

"Susan's sister told me this afternoon. Susan got pregnant in college and gave Alyson up for adoption."

"You're sure about this?"

Jack's stomach dropped.

Could Emily be deceiving you?

"You think she's lying?" Jack asked.

"I take nothing for granted." Reggie appeared to think of something then trotted up the stairs.

Jack found him in the hallway comparing Alyson's picture to their wedding picture.

"The likeness is amazing." Reggie rubbed his jaw. "Let's say this is true. If so, it changes things."

"In a good way?"

"We need to agree on three things before I take his case." Reggie stood in front of Jack, looking down from that three-inch advantage.

"And they are?"

"One, you tell me everything you find out as soon as you do. Two, you don't follow up on any leads without checking with me first."

"What's the third?"

"Whatever I say goes."

"That's fine."

"You sure you don't want to think about it?" Reggie looked at him. "I'm serious, Jack. I'm not into head games."

"I know you're not, and as far as thinking about it goes, I already have. It's what I expected you to say."

You actually sound sincere.

Reggie seemed to be thinking this over.

"So what do we do next?" Jack asked.

The private investigator looked into the distance. Something seemed to click.

"Let's go see John Walker," he said.

"You think he knows something?" Jack felt adrenaline move through him, his mind sharpening, fingers tingling.

"I think there's more to this story. Maybe he knows it, maybe he doesn't. Either way, I'll know after we talk to him."

Reggie's cell phone rang. He picked up. When he heard who it was he put his hand over the mouthpiece and excused himself.

Jack went into the kitchen. He tried using a rag to clean his pants, but it was useless.

Five minutes later, Reggie walked in.

"That was Rhonda, the detective in charge of Alyson's case. She just got a call. Someone claims they saw Alyson coming out of a rooming house on the East Side. Rhonda's in the midst of a homicide investigation and asked if I'd check it out."

"You mean now?" Jack asked.

"You've got something more important to do?"

"No."

"Then let's go, partner. I've got the address."

CHAPTER 16

NORMALLY, JACK WOULD'VE PREFERRED the way Reggie drove. He didn't exceed the speed limit. He didn't run red lights and came to a full stop at stop signs. But the half-hour it took them to get to the rooming house seemed interminable. It was two blocks from the Sound View River, in what had been a middle class neighborhood before those families moved north.

Reggie pulled his big black Buick into a parking space next to a schoolyard where a full-court basketball game was in progress. There were shouts. The ball against a backboard. Louder shouts and a rush toward the other team's basket accompanied by pounding that was louder in Jack's head than on the asphalt.

"Why are we parking here?" Jack asked as they got out. They had driven past two spaces that were closer.

"Rather they not know what my car looks like," Reggie pushed his remote. It beeped, the Buick locked safe and sound. "You mind walking?"

"Not at all," Jack said, wondering who "they" were.

The sun was a big orange ball, the sky turning red as they made their way up a long city block with crumbling brownstones lined up on the side opposite the basketball court.

Jack tripped on a crack in the sidewalk. Reggie grabbed his arm.

"Thanks."

"No problem."

An old woman wearing a bandana leaned out a third-story window with a pillow wedged under her elbows. Three little boys in cut-off shorts soaked themselves from an open fire hydrant, squealing, screaming obscenities about the water's frigid temperature. Two old men leaning against a beat-up Ford stopped talking when Jack and Reggie passed. A teenage girl wearing wraparound sunglasses and a low-cut halter walked past them listening to her iPod as if they didn't exist.

Could Alyson be living here?

"What's that saying about a red sky?" Jack asked.

"You mean red sky at night, sailor's delight; red sky in morning, sailor's warning?"

"You're sure it's not the other way around?"

"You nervous, Jack?"

"Not as long as you're not."

"I'm always nervous, I just never show it."

People sat on the concrete steps in front of the brownstones. A few made eye contact with Reggie, who nodded when they did.

"You don't want to be here when it gets dark," Reggie said.

You don't want to be here now. RUN!

"You know this area?" Jack tripped on another crack but regained his balance immediately.

"I grew up near here." Reggie looked around. "It wasn't this bad then."

"That's comforting."

A red Chevy Impala crawled past them. Its windows were tinted black, bass thumping.

"Here's how we play this," Reggie said. "I do the talking, you listen."

"I prefer it that way."

"Bull."

"I'm out of my element here, Reggie." Jack held up his hands.

"Glad to hear it. This could be the beginning of a beautiful friendship."

"Huh?"

"It's the last line of *Casablanca.*"

"Oh."

Reggie chuckled. "Jack, you need to get out more."

Two men in their twenties sat on the front steps of 143 Harbor Avenue. It had a red door and the address in black numbers on top of the sill. The men, not tall but muscular, wore long, baggy pants and no shirts.

"Either of you know which apartment the landlord lives in?" Reggie asked.

They looked at each other. One started laughing.

"Excuse me." Reggie had his hands on his hips. "I didn't tell a joke, I asked a question."

They looked Reggie up and down.

What have you gotten yourself into?

"You hear that, Barry? This man is asking us a question," the really short one said. He had a red dragon tattooed on his chest. "What you want coming here with your fancy suit and skinny friend?"

Jack looked into the dragon's eyes and shivered.

"I'm a private investigator. I'm looking for someone." Reggie pulled out a picture of Alyson. It was the same as the one on the postcard, only larger. "Have you seen her?"

"No," the tattooed one said, not looking at the picture.

That dragon's watching you.

"What about you, Barry?" Reggie held up the picture to him.

Barry stood up. His pants fell below his waist, exposing the waistband on his Tommy Hilfiger underwear.

Reggie said, "I'm just here to do my job, trying to help someone."

"Well we don't have a job and don't feel like helping anyone," the tattooed one said. He noticed Jack staring at his chest. "What you looking at?"

"Chill, Carlos," Barry said. "I know this PI." He turned to Reggie. "Your brother's Raymond, right?"

"Yeah," Reggie said.

"We used to play ball. His jump shot was def." Barry looked down the street and slid his hands into his pockets. "Just couldn't stay away from the white stuff." Barry pulled out half a cigarette and lit it, held it with his index finger curled around it.

Reggie stared at the sidewalk.

"I ain't seen that girl around." Smoke streamed from Barry's mouth. "My aunt's in apartment 1A. She's the landlord, you can ask her."

"Thanks." Reggie headed up the steps, Jack close behind.

"Your friend stays here." Carlos crossed his arms and blocked Reggie's path. The dragon peeked over Carlo's wrist.

Reggie looked at Barry.

"He's cool." Barry waved a hand. "Let them go in."

"I don't like the way this one keeps looking at me." Carlos pointed to Jack with his chin. "Latisha's in there and I don't trust this dude. Something wrong with him."

Jack's leg was shaking. The dragon was growling.

Reggie better not leave you with this lunatic.

Reggie was about to say something when the front door opened and a woman in her forties stuck her head out.

"Can I help you?" She was thin and short with tangled dark hair. "I'm the landlady."

"I'm a private investigator." Reggie trotted up the steps. She stepped outside and closed the door behind her. He showed her the picture of Alyson. "This missing girl was seen coming out of this building."

"I've never seen her." She shrugged. "I only rent to men. Most are old."

"And they stink," Carlos said.

"This girl wouldn't be with any of my tenants." The landlady shook her head.

Carlos laughed, holding his belly.

"Come on, Ester, couldn't you see Ramos hooking up with her?" His face turned serious. He looked at Reggie. "What's your name?"

"Reggie. Reggie Murphy."

Barry stuck out his hand. They shook brother style.

"A black Irishman," Carlos said. "Now that's funny."

"Carlos is good people," Barry said.

"I know." Reggie looked over his shoulder. "He just can't help messing with suits. That right, Carlos?"

"Don't analyze me, Sigmund. Your friend here, he's the one needs his head shrunk."

Reggie gave Ester and Barry his business card.

"How come I don't get one?" Carlos's hands were pistols pointed at his chest. The dragon didn't flinch.

"Cause you'll just tear it up," Reggie said.

"You got that right."

"If you see her, I'd appreciate your giving me a call," Reggie said to Ester.

"I'll do that, Mr. Murphy."

"I will do that, Mr. Murphy," Carlos said. "I can't listen to this crap any longer." He went down the steps and started walking toward where Reggie had parked. "Tell Latisha I be back soon and she better be ready to go."

"Excuse me," Barry said. "I got to talk to him." He tossed his cigarette and caught up with Carlos. They leaned against a car. Barry was talking, Carlos was shaking his head.

Ester sighed and went inside.

Reggie stood next to Jack and looked around.

"What do you make of it?" Jack asked.

"Some leads work out. This one didn't. It's as simple as that."

Jack looked down the block, opposite where Carlos and Barry had gone. He saw what looked like a blond girl coming toward them. His pulse raced. She had on baggy pants, a black tee shirt, and a Yankee cap. He poked Reggie.

"Is that Alyson?"

She was still half a block away when she looked up, stopped short, turned and ran.

"Alyson!" Jack yelled.

She didn't stop.

He went after her.

"Jack!" Reggie took off after him.

Jack kept running, gaining speed with each stride, his mind focused on the girl ahead of him.

She went left.

He followed her down an alley. At the end of it he came to rows of back yards separated by chain-link fences.

"Alyson!" Jack shouted, his breathing labored. "ALYSON!"

She hopped over one fence, then another.

Reggie was no longer behind him.

You're on your own.

Jack made it over the first fence, ran to the second, his lungs burning, his heart hammering his chest. He pushed himself up and over, cutting his hand in the process.

Alyson went over the third fence and darted out of the backyard.

Jack tore his pants going over that fence.

He ran down the alley Alyson had taken—

And came to a full stop. A young boy with long blond hair and a Yankee cap under his arm was standing in front of Carlos.

"You finally made it," Carlos said. The boy was out of breath. Barry sat on a milk carton, off to the side. Reggie was next to him, also out of breath.

Jack was panting, his hand bleeding. Reggie came over to him.

"Are you all right?"

Jack nodded, eying the boy with blond hair.

"You're surprised to see a white boy in this neighborhood," Carlos said.

"It's not that, it's just I was sure she…I mean he was—"

"Save it." Carlos showed him a palm and looked out the corner of his eye. "Told you, Barry, this dude's a certified nut."

Barry stood up. His pants fell below his waist again.

"Aw, he thought Mo was the girl they looking for, that's all, honest mistake. Stupid, but honest."

"I ain't so sure about that," Carlos said. "But let's say it's true. Mo, how you feel about him thinking you're a girl?"

"I want you to kick his ass." Mo put his baseball cap on backwards.

"Don't touch him," Reggie said through his teeth.

"This says he can." Mo lifted his tee shirt and tapped the butt of a pistol shoved in his pants.

"That's not real," Reggie said.

"Want to find out for sure?" Carlos grinned.

Reggie snorted but didn't move.

Barry spread his arms wide. "Carlos, you want to go to jail for something as stupid as this?"

"Go to jail for what? Beating the dude up?" He stepped closer to Jack, then nodded at Reggie. "No one's gonna get shot long as he keeps out of it." He pushed Jack. "Come on, chump, hit me, it's the only chance you got."

Jack balled his hands, kept them at his sides.

Carlos punched him in the gut.

Jack doubled over, air whooshing from his lungs. The dragon

was watching him, eyes seething, mouth open, ready to strike. Jack lunged at it.

Kill it.

Carlos stepped aside and threw an uppercut. Reggie grabbed his wrist before the punch reached Jack's jaw.

"That's enough," Reggie said, twisting Carlos's arm behind him.

"Let go of me!"

"I will as soon as you stop this."

Reggie shoved Carlos, who stumbled. Reggie grabbed Mo's gun and looked at it, shaking his head.

"They did a nice job of making it look real." He tossed the pistol to Carlos.

"Come on, let's get out of here," Barry said with his hand on Mo's back, moving him along. Carlos gave Jack a long stare before he followed the other two up the alley.

"Sorry, Reggie," Jack said when they were out of earshot. "I was sure he was Alyson."

"You didn't hear me calling you?"

"All I could think about was catching up to her, I mean him."

"You need to control yourself, Jack. This is a serious business. You do something stupid again and you can find yourself another private investigator."

He's letting you off easy.

"I appreciate your stepping in like that." Jack examined his bloody hand.

"How'd you cut yourself?"

"When I jumped that fence." Jack pointed.

Reggie pulled the handkerchief from his front breast pocket and tossed it to him. "You can keep that."

"It's silk, you sure?"

"Rather you ruin that than get blood on my car's upholstery. You do that and you'll really piss me off."

"Thanks." Jack wrapped the handkerchief around the cut. He

looked around. "How'd you know he'd wind up here? Which by the way, is where?"

"We're in the back yard of the rooming house. Told you I grew up not far from here. I know all the tricks. You took a pretty good punch; did he hurt you?"

"I'm fine." Jack tied the handkerchief.

"So you're going to Nestor tomorrow with Emily?"

"You think it's crazy?"

"It's worth a shot," Reggie said. "Sometimes you learn what you need to where you least expect."

"I'll be back on Sunday."

"Good. By then I'll know if John Walker can meet with us on Monday." Reggie sighed. "Come on, let's get out of here. I've had enough of this place."

Jack had too.

CHAPTER 17

THE NEXT EVENING JACK accelerated onto the thruway at six-fifteen. The sky was pale blue as the sun began its slow descent on the left. Tree-covered mountains rose in the distance. He was driving the middle lane, his hands on the wheel at eight and four. It was Saturday. Traffic was light. The weekend crowd had left yesterday.

Emily was in the passenger seat wearing a short, sleeveless red dress. She said they had a two-hour drive ahead of them. He took her word for it—he'd never been to the small upstate town of Nestor.

Emily's hand hung out the window. No one had ever smoked in Jack's car, but he was making an exception—with three conditions. Allowing the cigarette in the car only to take a drag on it was the first.

"So what's the plan?" Jack asked as they passed a sign that read: Nestor 90 miles. Emily had promised to answer any questions on the ride up when she told him yesterday to be ready at six with a full tank of gas and an overnight bag.

"We're going to see Eleanor Ridge, Susan's college room-mate. She owns a bar." Emily swept blowing hair away from her face. "Alan likes to go there."

"How do you know that?"

"Susan told me."

"How did she know?" His muscles tightened.

Emily shrugged. "She probably found out from Eleanor. They had lunch together whenever Eleanor came home to visit her mother."

"Does Eleanor know about Alyson?"

"Only you and I know." Emily gave him a hard look. "Don't screw that up."

"I got it." He recalled his mistake yesterday thinking Mo was Alyson, his stomach still sore from Carlos's punch. "What else do you know about Alan Dean?"

"As of two years ago he was still an English professor at Whitmore College and still married to the same woman he left Susan for." Emily pulled in her cigarette, took a quick drag on it, and shoved it back out the window again.

Jack tilted his head from side to side, trying to crack the tension in his neck that intensified with each revelation.

Emily shot smoke out the side of her mouth, and most of it made it out the window. He was impressed. That was the second condition he'd set for smoking in his car, and so far she'd kept to that one too.

A minivan with two teenage girls peering out the back window slid in front of them. The girls looked like twins. They smiled and waved. Emily waved back.

"You ever meet Alan?" Jack asked.

"No. I moved back from California just before Susan got pregnant." Emily flicked her cigarette. Its ash flew out the window. "Of course, not having met him doesn't stop me from having an opinion of him."

"Which is?"

"He's a self-centered prick." She let out a long breath. Not as much smoke made it outside this time. Jack twitched.

"Maybe it was because Susan had to give up Alyson," she said. "Maybe it was Alan dumping her for another woman after they were engaged. The bottom line is—"

"Wait a second, they were engaged?"

"You didn't know?"

Jack swerved left.

A horn honked.

He swerved right.

"Look out!" Emily shouted.

He was inches from a black jeep in the right lane. Its horn blared. Jack turned the wheel and regained control of his car. The Jeep sped ahead of them. Its driver glared at Jack.

How could Susan not tell you she was engaged?

Jack checked his rearview mirror. Police lights were flashing. His stomach dropped.

"Are you all right?" Emily asked.

"There's a trooper behind us. We're being pulled over."

Emily looked out the rear window. "This is the last thing we needed."

"I'll handle it." Jack eased off the gas and maneuvered onto the shoulder, his heart beating wildly. He stopped the car, rammed the shift into park, lowered his window.

The police car parked behind him, lights still flashing.

Jack's hands were shaking. He squeezed the wheel tighter. His hands shook more.

Emily sighed, checked her watch, and turned around.

"I'm going to find out what's going on." She reached for the door handle.

"No you're not." Jack held her door shut. "They always want you to stay in the car. I'll take it from here."

You think you can?

Emily was about to say something, then crossed her arms and leaned back in her seat.

"Suit yourself."

The state trooper got out of the cruiser and walked towards him. Jack watched her shiny black boots in his side-view mirror. She reached his car and leaned in.

"Do you know why I pulled you over?" Her nametag said Brady. She was stout and muscular, with short dark hair. Her hand was on the open window. She had stubby fingers and dirt under her nails.

Jack clutched his neck as if choking himself.

"Is something wrong?" Brady asked.

"I just found out my wife had been engaged to someone else." Jack straightened his collar. His voice rose as he suppressed an urge to tell the cop the entire story right from the beginning.

Tell her. Do it. DO IT.

The trooper was wearing mirrored sunglasses.

"Officer, this is my fault." Emily leaned forward. "I was just—"

"Ma'am, were you driving?" Brady pushed up her hat and stuck her head in the car. She reeked of perspiration. Jack felt nauseous.

"No, officer," Emily said.

"I said I'll handle this," Jack said through clenched teeth.

"Well, you're not doing a very good job of it," Emily said under her breath.

"Please give me your license and registration," Brady said. Jack reached into his wallet and handed them to her. "Where are you heading?"

"To Nestor," Jack said.

"You teach at Whitmore?"

Jack almost said he did, thinking maybe Brady had a niece who wanted to attend college there. But he couldn't risk getting caught in a lie.

Who cares? Come on, say it. SAY IT.

"We're setting up a scholarship." Emily pointed to Jack. "It's in his late wife's name. She was my sister."

"Sir, I'd like you step out of the car." Brady moved away from the door.

Jack stuck his head out the window. "Officer, what's this about?"

"You were driving erratically." Her hand hovered over her gun. "Now please step out of your vehicle."

"I just swerved out of my lane," Jack said. "No harm, no foul." Surely she had a serial killer to catch, maybe even a terrorist or two. "I'm a tax-paying citizen, in the highest bracket—"

"Mr. Logan, you're trying my patience."

"Jack, please call me Jack. All my employees do."

Brady pulled in a deep breath and groaned.

"Okay, okay." Jack opened the door and got out.

What a humorless bitch.

"Have you been drinking, Mr. Logan?"

Other vehicles passed by, their occupants rubbernecking, no doubt grateful they weren't in his predicament.

Jack pointed to himself. "I haven't had a drink all day, officer."

"You willing to take a sobriety test?"

Hot wind hit Jack's face. His knees felt weak.

Damn.

Across the highway a red Cadillac convertible was parked on the shoulder. Two men were in the front seat, both unshaven. They needed a good scrubbing. A young woman was in the back seat. Her hands were behind her back.

"Officer, that woman, she's tied up." Jack pointed, just as the woman stretched her arms over her head.

"She is not." Brady said. "What are you talking about?"

"Never mind." Jack hit the side of his head.

"Are you willing to take a sobriety test?"

"Sure." He began to sweat. He hated tests.

"Good answer. Please count backwards from one hundred."

Jack squinted. "You mean here, now?" He bowed his head. "Of course you do."

"Now that we've got that settled, start counting."

Jack's body tensed. His jaw locked. He couldn't speak.

You're screwed.

"Is there a problem?" the trooper asked.

He heard the numbers in his mind, getting louder. He covered his ears.

"What are you doing?"

"Come on, baby you can do it," he heard Susan say. His mouth still couldn't move. His car door slammed.

"I'm sorry, Mr. Logan, you're going to have to—"

"Officer, this man's wife just died," Emily said as she approached and pointed at Jack. "He hasn't been drinking. I can vouch for that."

"Ma'am, please return to your vehicle."

"Didn't you hear what I just said?" Emily put her hands on her hips. "Have some compassion."

"Ma'am, if you don't get back in that car right now I'm going to arrest you for obstruction."

Jack still couldn't speak.

What's wrong with you?

Emily blew out a breath and walked back to the Mercedes, looking over her shoulder every other step.

"Mr. Logan, I'm giving you one more chance." The trooper's back was to Jack's car. Jack saw Emily in the front seat, mouthing the numbers he needed to recite.

"One hundred….ninety-nine….ninety-eight, ninety-seven," Jack began. The words came out faster as he went along.

"Okay, you can stop now," the trooper said after seventy-nine. She handed him back his license and registration. "Be more careful next time."

"That's it?" Jack took the documents from her.

"You want a summons for reckless driving?" Brady peered in at him.

"No. No. Thanks." Jack held up his hands. "I don't want a summons."

The trooper took off her sunglasses and stepped closer. She had peanut on her breath.

Tell her, her breath stinks. TELL HER.

"Don't ever let a passenger distract you." Brady looked toward Emily. "Especially that one."

"I hear you, officer." Jack saluted her.

Brady donned her sunglasses and headed back to the cruiser. Jack got in his car and shut the door.

"You just can't listen, can you?" he said as he clicked his seatbelt.

Emily didn't say anything, for which he was grateful.

Jack's head was pounding as he waited for the trooper to pull out. After she did, he got back on the thruway.

They had driven a mile in silence when he asked, "You started to say that Susan was never—"

"Apologize," Emily said.

"Apologize for what?"

"You were being a dick back there, Jack."

"How was I a dick?"

"Oh, let's see. How about 'I'll handle this,'" she said.

"You're serious?"

"Yes. Now apologize."

"I did. I do."

"You don't sound sincere."

"You're pushing your luck," Jack said.

More silence, which Emily finally broke.

"As I was saying, Susan was never the same after Alan Dean came into her life and left it."

"What was she like before?"

"She was fun, spontaneous—adventurous. She didn't care what color she wore."

The Susan you never met. Would she have loved you?

"I thought the change in her would pass. It never did."

"You said Alan is still married to the woman he left Susan for." Jack slid his eyes toward Emily. "Maybe he really loves her."

"See how little you know, Logan. His wife is rich."

"So you're a pessimist?"

"Selling real estate teaches you a lot about human nature, Jack. Sometimes more than you want to know. There are all kinds of people out there. Some are real shits and I'd be willing to bet Alan Dean was and still is as shitty as they come."

"You could be wrong."

"You'll find out." She smiled.

She knows something you don't.

Emily brought her hand back inside the car. The cigarette was gone. It bothered him that she littered, but he'd given her no other choice. His third condition for her smoking in his car was that she not use the ashtray.

"It was good Susan had you to confide in," he said.

"She only told me about Alyson because I had a place for her to stay until the baby was born."

"You and Susan weren't close back then?"

"No."

"Why?"

"I'd say it's because I'm a bitch." Emily looked out her window. "I could tell you the reason I'm this way is because my mother died in childbirth and my father still resents me for it, that Susan's mother never made me feel like I was her daughter. But all that's just an excuse to ruin your life." Emily wrapped her arms around herself. "I'm not always proud of the way I am, but it works, at least it does for me." She looked down. "The only thing I've ever needed is someone I can trust and confide in. I wanted that to be Susan, but she could never feel close to me."

"She told you that?"

"Her actions did." Emily crossed her legs. Her feet were bare, her soles were dirty. He shuddered. She reached into her pocketbook and pulled out the directions for the last leg of their trip.

"You know anything else?" Jack asked.

"Only that there's more to the story." They approached a sign that said: Welcome to Nestor. Emily tapped her window, her nails clicking against the glass. "And I'm sure some of it's right here."

CHAPTER 18

"I TAKE IT WE'RE GOING straight to Eleanor's."

"You've got a better idea?" Emily was looking at the directions.

They'd been driving for two hours. The sun had nearly set. Jack couldn't wait to get out of the car, stretch his legs, use the restroom.

"You ever meet Eleanor?" he said.

"Once, a long time ago, but it won't be hard to find her." Emily's arm shot out to the side. "Turn right at that light." She looked at him. "If she's there, you'll know it."

The first thing Jack saw when they walked into Eleanor's was a big woman with long platinum blond hair behind the bar, holding two mugs and pulling on a tap. She had to be six feet tall. She wasn't overweight but had broad shoulders, large breasts, and bulging biceps. Her brown eyes were in constant motion.

She handed the mugs to one employee, winked at another, and pointed to a customer—all done effortlessly. Jack had no doubt this was Eleanor Ridge. She wasn't just someone who'd own a bar; she was someone who'd name it after herself.

The place was half full with an even mix of men and women, most somewhere in their twenties. Music blasted from a jukebox on the wall opposite the bar—the passionate singer yearning for more. The dance floor in front of the jukebox was empty. A young man ran one of the pool tables in back while his opponent tapped the floor with the butt of his cue. Two attractive women on the other table laughed and high-fived.

Jack and Emily found two seats at the bar.

Eleanor dropped two coasters in front of them. She looked at Emily and narrowed her eyes.

"I know you?" Eleanor's voice was softer than Jack had expected.

"I'm Emily White, Susan's sister." Emily nodded at him. "Jack Logan, Susan's husband."

"Good lord!" Eleanor put her hand on Emily's. "I'm so sorry, I just heard last month." She looked at Jack. "Your wife was a good friend. I hadn't talked to her in two years—something I regret."

"My sister was fond of you," Emily said.

Eleanor smiled. She had perfect teeth.

"What would you like to drink?" she asked as she washed a cocktail glass.

Is that rag she's using clean?

"I'll have a vodka martini," Emily said, "and make it dirty."

"Please make my mine clean." Jack shivered. "Make it immaculate."

"You got it." Eleanor stepped away but was back in no time with their drinks. "So what brings you to Nestor?"

Is that a fingerprint on the rim of your glass?

"We'd like to establish a scholarship in Susan's name," Emily said, "and Jack has never seen Whitmore's campus."

They liked the scholarship idea so much they'd decided to actually do it.

"We also hoped to see you." Emily put her hand on Jack's arm. He twitched. "Jack asked me what Susan was like in college. I thought you'd have more memories than I do."

"We were roommates." Eleanor waved off Jack's attempt to pay for the drinks. "We had a lot of good times together."

"Emily says Susan was a bit of a rebel." Jack lowered his eyes. "She wasn't that way with me."

"Well, now, Susie was different the first half of college." Eleanor leaned against the counter behind her and crossed her muscular arms.

Susie?

"I remember once we just started an all-nighter for a history midterm the next day," Eleanor said. "She says, 'Screw the Battle of Hastings. We're going on a road trip.'" Eleanor opened a bottle of beer and placed it in front of the man next to Emily. "That was Susie."

Jack tried to picture the scene but couldn't. He'd never seen that Susan.

And now you never will.

He spun his martini glass, studying it, imagining the germs on the glass gathering their forces, preparing to attack.

Eleanor snatched an empty beer mug from the bar and began washing it.

Is she not using soap?

"After we were no longer roommates, we were still close, but she was more withdrawn." Eleanor's face looked sad.

"Do you know why?" he asked.

"It started after Alan Dean left her." Eleanor dried the mug she'd just washed.

"Alan Dean, is he the college professor?" Jack said.

"That's the one." Eleanor looked at the clock above her. "As a matter of fact, he usually stops by for a drink Saturdays around nine." She excused herself to give change to a pool player.

Jack's eyes darted from side to side. "Let's get out of here," he said under his breath.

"We haven't even talked to him," Emily said. "Don't you—"

"Not without giving some thought to what we're going to say first." His hands were shaking. He started to sweat. Someone howled. The two women were now playing pool with the men. The song on jukebox ended and another came on.

"We'll keep it simple," Emily said. "We just need to find out what kind of person he is."

"We can come back next weekend—after we've had a chance to plan it out." Jack stole a glance at the door.

"Bull. It's a long drive. This is our opportunity. We've got to take advantage of it." She leaned closer, vodka on her breath. "We've got to do this for Susan—and for Alyson."

"There he is now." Eleanor nodded toward the entrance as she filled a mug with ale.

The clock above the bar read 9:02. Alan was punctual—

And he had black curly hair, a thin straight nose, deep-set eyes. Blood rushed to Jack's face.

"He looks like me."

Where does this end?

"So he does." Emily smiled and shook her head.

At least there was one noticeable difference: Alan had a pot belly. He carried it well, about as well as you could carry such a thing. Jack patted his stomach, grateful it was still flat. Now he had one more reason to keep it that way.

Alan walked to the bar.

Damn.

The crowd was thicker now, but Jack felt as if they were the only ones there. The music sounded louder.

Jack snuck out his sanitizer and rubbed some into his hands.
You know this can only turn out bad.
Seconds slipped by. Alan kept walking. When a young man
called his name he stopped, smiled, and waved. Then he con-
tinued toward the bar.
You're trapped.
Alan was only a few steps away. Destiny was having its say.
It didn't give a shit about Jack Logan.
"Hello Alan," Emily said when he reached the bar. Her voice
was steady, even relaxed.
She gets better as the stakes get higher.
Alan turned towards her as if he'd been tapped on the
shoulder.
"Do I know you?" he asked.
"I'm Emily White."
"Susan White's sister?"
"That would be me." Emily smiled that smile. The one that
said she was in control of the situation and would keep it that
way. She jabbed her thumb over her shoulder. "This is Jack
Logan, my brother-in-law. Susan's husband."
Alan's face reddened.
Jack nodded, his leg shaking. Suddenly confronting Carlos
yesterday didn't seem so bad.
"I was…" Alan gulped air. "I was so sorry to hear about
Susan." He looked at Eleanor, who barely shrugged. "I was very
sad when I heard…." Alan closed his eyes. "Very sad."
"You want the usual?" Eleanor asked him.
He nodded.
The man sitting next to Emily left with his beer. Alan stared
at the empty barstool as if it might explode. He stuck out his
hand to Jack.
"My condolences." He didn't make eye contact.
Jack shook his hand but couldn't speak.
He's got to see the resemblance.

Jack was sure Alan's forehead was higher than his. There *were* differences. Just not as many as Jack wanted.

"Emily and Jack are setting up a scholarship in Susan's name," Eleanor said as she wiped down the bar in front of Alan.

"You mean at Whitmore?"

"No better place," Emily said. "Jack hasn't seen the campus. That's why we're here."

"You were there today?" Alan narrowed his eyes.

"We're going tomorrow." Jack was finally able to speak.

Alan's gaze moved from Eleanor to Jack to Emily, then back to Jack again.

"I'm on the scholarship committee." He sighed. "I'll be in my office tomorrow...until noon." He appeared to weigh something. "Stop by if you have any questions."

Emily better have a plan.

Alan leaned past her. He seemed to recognize something.

Is it that you look alike?

"Your wife was a special person," Alan said.

"Yes she was." Jack eyed the door. More people were coming, crowding him in.

There's no way out.

"How long were you married?"

"Two years." Jack shuddered. Alan had also had two years with Susan.

"Everyone liked her." Alan raised his glass as if making a toast. "There was never a dull moment when she was around."

The music was loud. It was difficult to hear.

Emily shoved her thumb at Jack. "He met her and never let her go."

Alan leaned back and bumped the attractive brunette standing behind him.

"I'm sorry," he said.

The young woman turned around, annoyed, then smiled when she saw who it was.

"Sometimes your life is heading in one direction, then goes in another," Alan said to no one in particular. He seemed to be studying the liquor bottles lined up at the back of the bar.

Emily handed Eleanor her empty glass. "A refill, please." The music stopped in the middle of a love song.

Emily turned to Alan. "My sister was never the same after you left her. I need to know why."

"It appears you don't like me," Alan said. "Anything I say about your sister—"

"Just tell me the truth." Emily propped her cheek on her fist. "That might change my opinion."

Alan finished his drink and slapped down the empty glass.

"Sorry, but I've got to go. It was nice meeting you two." He put a ten on the bar, waved to Eleanor, and slid off his stool.

Emily blocked his path.

"Tell me."

"Tell you *what*?"

"Why did you leave her?"

"So that's why you're here. The scholarship was just a ruse."

"It's not." Emily's fists pressed her sides. "Running into you here was a coincidence."

"There are no coincidences," Alan said.

"Maybe you're right." Emily lifted her chin. "Everything happens for a reason."

Alan turned to Jack. "What about you? Is this something you want to hear about too?"

Jack wanted to leave.

"I...yes."

"Don't say I didn't warn you." Alan sat back down and asked Eleanor for a refill. She brought him a rum and coke, placed a fresh martini in front of Emily, and asked Jack if he wanted anything. He wanted another drink. A double.

"No thanks, I'm good," Jack said.

Eleanor stepped away.

"Susie wanted a family. I didn't." Alan held a thin red straw between his palms. He crushed it. "That's what drove us apart."

Jack felt nauseous. The room was spinning.

He calls her Susie too? Is everyone who knew-her-when insane?

"You didn't discuss having children before you got engaged?" Jack grabbed onto the bar. Susie, Susan…he couldn't picture his wife with anyone but himself.

"She said having a family wasn't as important as being with me."

"So what was the problem?" Emily asked.

Alan sighed. "It wasn't true."

"You were also involved with someone else." Emily raised a finger. "Let's not forget that."

"Look, Susie isn't here to give her side of the story and you don't believe mine. Let's drop it."

"Just tell the truth." Emily was on the edge of her seat.

Alan looked at Jack. "Susie was—"

Jack pounded the top of the bar. "What's wrong with you people? She's Susan. Do you hear me? You call your teenage niece Susie. You call your pet terrier Susie. You call the woman I married Susan. Susan LOGAN. Understand?"

"You don't like your wife's nickname. I got it." Alan pursed his lips. "So let's say I overheard *Susan* say I'd eventually want a family, I just needed time to come around to the idea."

"You're saying she lied to you?" Jack balled his hands.

"Jack," Eleanor said. "He's telling the truth. She did think he'd eventually want kids. It was just one of those things that didn't work out." She held Jack's wrist. "Best leave it alone."

Jack uncurled his hands and rested them on the bar.

Emily finished her second martini.

"So you have kids now?" Jack asked.

"We have no desire to be parents." Alan stared at Jack as if he were a student who'd just missed the entire point of his lecture. "I thought it was wrong to feel that way. Then I met Michelle. We love our life and wouldn't change it for anything or any*one*."

"Too bad you didn't meet her before you met Susan," Emily said. "Everything would be so less complicated if you had."

Alan looked at her as if she'd just spit in his face. "You wanted the truth. I gave it to you."

"Your version of it."

Alan looked at his watch. "It's been a delightful encounter, but I've got to meet my wife." He put down another bill, said goodnight to Eleanor, and disappeared into the crowd.

Jack sat frozen.

"You okay?" Emily said.

"Never better."

He was imagining exactly what he'd do to Alan Dean if he were in the parking lot.

CHAPTER 19

AT ELEVEN P.M. HE AND EMILY entered the office of the Mountainside Motel, which Eleanor Ridge said was the best of the three motels in Nestor. That didn't say much for the other two.

Jack was so tired he could've kissed the middle-aged woman behind the tiny counter when she looked over her reading glasses and handed them each a key.

Now Jack and Emily were sitting out on a deck that ran along the second floor. The air was still and warm. Crickets were chirping. They were about to say goodnight.

Should you shake hands or hug?

When another couple squeezed past them, Emily got up.

"See you tomorrow," she said, and they each went inside their rooms.

Jack closed the door, slid on the chain, and drew the front window's thin curtains closed. He looked around the room. A floor lamp stood in the corner. A pre-flat-screen television sat on top of a veneer dresser. Reading lights hung over each of the two double beds. He ran a finger over the night table. No dust. That was a relief.

He put his overnight bag on the bed closest to the window.

What about bedbugs?

He stared at the other bed. The one he'd sleep in. He saw himself lying with his eyes closed while tiny hairy creatures covered him, sucking his blood. There was a padded chair in the corner. He couldn't sleep in that. His back was hurting, his body heavy. Knees felt weak. He took a deep breath and fell back on the bedspread. Any minute now he'd feel something crawling on his skin. His eyes closed. Sounds from Eleanor's rang in his ears.

The scene changed to a meadow.

Susan was floating above him, attached by a long cord—an umbilical cord? He reached for her as she drifted away toward a flaming sky. Carlos stood above him showing off his big white teeth while Mo shot a water pistol at him. "Don't go!" Jack tried to scream, but the words choked him. He pushed Carlos away and flew towards Susan. They touched, feeding their hunger for each other. They didn't speak, but he knew her thoughts and feelings. A fierce wind howled. Lighting flashed. Thunder clapped. Rain came down in torrents. Susan held him. "I love you, Jack." They were soaked, they came together and began falling, stars all around them. Then they were on their backs, staring at a red sun. "You have to let me go, Jack." Susan's lips didn't move. "Why?" He touched her cheek and burned his fingers. "She's dead." Carlos was standing over Jack. "Get over it, loon." "No. She's alive! Look at her." Reggie sat in a recliner, taking notes. "How does that make you feel?" Susan's blond hair turned red. "Don't screw this up." Jack looked at her, confused—her eyes were emerald green. "It's about to get harder," Emily said. She was wearing the black blouse Susan had on the day she died. "Together we can do it," Emily said. "Trust me." He looked over at Reggie—

Someone was knocking at the door of his room.

Someone knocked harder.

Jack bolted upright, clicked on the reading lamp, and checked the clock on the nightstand. Midnight. He'd been asleep for a half-hour.

He opened the door and saw his wife's sister barefoot, still in her red dress. It had gold buttons down the front, the top two now open. She looked good in it. Jack's face felt warm. Emily glanced at his bare chest—his white button-down shirt was open. He buttoned it, tucked it in, and buckled his belt.

She had two glasses in one hand and a silver flask in the other.

"Don't tell me you want to have a drink."

"I can't sleep. I'm too wired." She held up the flask. "This usually helps." She smiled at him. "Can you get some ice?"

She walked in. He grabbed the ice bucket off the dresser and shoved the room key into his pocket.

"Be right back."

He headed down the stairs, a few remnants of the dream still swirling in his brain.

He found the ice machine off a narrow hallway and jammed the bucket under its spout. Ice cubes rattled out like bullets spraying from an Uzi. Once the bucket was full, he went back up the stairs, two at a time.

He stopped outside the door to his room.

The dream had left him vulnerable. But he and Emily would not sleep together, he was sure of that. At least, he was sure if she was sure, and he was pretty sure she was.

He entered the room and met Emily's big green eyes. She was sitting on the bed. He locked the door and handed her the ice bucket. She picked through the cubes.

"Big, Jack. I only like them big."

She dropped six that met her expectations into two crystal tumblers.

"You brought your own glasses?"

"The glass is almost as important as what you put in it." Emily unscrewed the cap of the flask. Her auburn hair fell over her shoulder as she poured a light brown liquid into each glass. Ice cracked. She picked up his glass by the rim and handed it to him.

He passed it under his nose, trying to figure out where he could put his lips that her fingers hadn't touched.

"Here's to Susan." Emily raised her drink.

Their glasses clinked. Emily downed a third of hers. He forced the glass to his mouth and tipped it. The scotch bit the back of his throat and warmed his stomach. Soon he felt lighter. He drank more, forgetting about Emily's fingers.

She hadn't brought her cigarettes. She'd probably want one sooner or later. Maybe she'd use that as a reason to leave—a means of escape in case she needed one. He wondered if she'd left the cigarettes on purpose.

Jack sat on the edge of the bed, Emily leaned against the headboard. She stretched out her legs. The soles of her dirty feet grazed his leg.

He flinched.

"You didn't want to talk to Alan." Emily's toe poked his thigh. "Weren't you curious?"

"You're good at dealing with people, I'm not."

Emily grabbed her ankles and slid closer to him.

"Having you there helped." She touched his arm. He felt a chill. "You gave me confidence."

"I never saw you as someone who lacked that."

"I'm not as self-assured as people think." Emily rose and stepped off the bed as if it were a cliff. She stood in front of him. The lamp behind her framed her hair in light, an auburn halo. "Excuse me, I need to use the bathroom." She walked past him and shut the door behind her.

Maybe you can trust her.

He pictured the door opening, Emily standing there. No words between them. She takes a step, one foot in front of the other. His heart is pounding. She reaches him. He's frozen, confused. Her hand slips behind his head and draws him closer. Their lips meet. The kiss lingers. He wants to pull away, wants to run. But she's forgiven him for what he did to Susan. He can't lose that. Emily steps back and bows her head. She looks up. She's Susan.

Jack buried his face in his hands. "No…it's too soon for that."

There was a click. Emily emerged from the bathroom.

"So what do you think of the professor?" Emily plopped down next to him. He felt the heat coming off her.

"What do I think…what?"

"Alan," Emily said. "Alan Dean."

"He makes me nauseous." He clasped the back of his neck. "What did Susan see in him?"

"I'm more certain than ever that if—no, *when*—we find Alyson we shouldn't tell her about him." Emily leaned back on her elbows.

"He's her father—a jerk, but *he's still her* FATHER."

"He doesn't want to be a father. Tonight he made that abundantly clear."

"I won't lie to Alyson." Jack shuddered. "I'll never do that. I'll never call my wife Susie and I'll never lie to Alyson." He felt his eyes bulge. "You understand?"

"I want what's best for her." Emily stared at the ceiling.

"What are you looking at?" Jack panicked. "You see a bedbug?"

"Where, on the ceiling?"

Jack shrugged.

"We talk about Alyson as if we know nothing bad has happened to her," Emily said.

"She's fine." Jack's voice boomed.

"It sounds like you know how this story ends."

"Not yet, but I'll figure it out." He smiled. "Alyson will go to Whitmore. She'll be the first recipient of the Susan Logan scholarship."

"Jack, I don't want her anywhere near Alan Dean."

"We have to tell Alyson about him," Jack said. "We can't keep that from her."

"What if Alan refuses to meet her?" Emily raised an eyebrow. "He very well might, and if he does, Alyson would be rejected—again. That's not happening on my watch."

"How about this?" Jack sat up. "Tomorrow we tell Alan about Alyson. At least we know where he is."

Emily's expression said she didn't like the idea, but she was quiet for a minute. "Okay," she said finally. "On one condition."

"And that is?"

"If he doesn't want to meet her, we don't tell Alyson about him."

He'll want to meet his only child.

"Fine," Jack said.

"Good."

You shouldn't have agreed to this. You know you won't keep to it if he—

"Wait." Jack held up his hands. "I'm sorry, I can't agree to that."

"Jack!"

"I didn't say won't, I said can't. I'm just being honest."

"Doesn't matter." Emily swatted the air with the back of her hand. "Once you see his reaction, you won't want her near him anyway."

She's letting you off easy. Probably has something up her sleeve.

"Now all I have to do is find Alyson."

"We'll find her, Jack. It'll be balls to the wall right after we leave Whitmore."

WE'LL find her? Emily would help him find Alyson? Of course she would. She was her aunt.

You need all the help you can get.

Jack got off the bed and stood in front of her.

Emily looked up at him. "Mind doing me a favor?"

"No more money for you!" Jack wagged a finger.

"No." Emily chuckled. "Let me give you a hug."

"I can do that."

She wrapped her arms around him and held him tight. He recalled her saying she needed someone she could trust and confide in. He needed that too.

Emily let go and stepped back.

"Thanks." She grabbed her glass and flask. "I'll see you in the morning." Then she left.

CHAPTER 20

Robert Frost Hall was quiet on a Saturday morning. The door to Alan Dean's office was ajar. He was seated at his desk, reading.

Jack knocked. His pulse was racing. Telling Alan Dean about Alyson had been his idea, but at the moment it felt like a really bad one.

You can't do this.

He was glad Emily was next to him.

"Come in." Alan had on a blue knit shirt and reading glasses halfway down his nose.

Emily shut the door behind them. Alan looked at them like they were IRS auditors.

The English professor had a large office, but the light yellow walls above the bookcases were bare except for two framed diplomas that hung behind his desk, which was stacked with piles of papers. Smaller stacks were scattered on top of a round table by a big window. Nothing seemed in order. Alan waved them into two club chairs across from the desk.

"So what did you think of the campus?" He opened his side drawer and pulled something out. "If you want to know how the scholarship will be administered, this manual should answer all your questions."

Jack thanked him, took the manual, then took the plunge.

"We...want to talk to you about something else." Jack rammed his hand deep into his pocket. "Something unrelated to the scholarship." He wiped perspiration from his forehead. His hands felt dirty. He'd forgotten his hand sanitizer.

"Why am I not surprised?" Alan said.

Jack studied the frayed green carpet. He rubbed his hands together.

"I guess...."

"You guess what?" Alan looked at him.

"I guess the best way is to just say it. Susan was pregnant when you broke up with her." He met Alan's steely gaze.

Shit, he really does look like you.

"Susan would never cheat on me."

"You're right," Emily said. "You may not like children, but you're a father."

Alan looked to his left, toward the window. It was open two inches. He got up, walked over, and shut it.

"You're mistaken. She'd have told me." He sat back down in his high-back black leather chair. It was the newest thing in the room.

"She didn't know—until right after you left her."

Jack watched his face cycle from incredulity to wariness to anger to confusion. This guy had better not play poker, he'd lose his shirt.

"Why are you telling me this?" he said.

"The woman who adopted her died three months ago," Jack said. He crossed his legs, uncrossed them, crossed them again. "Now—"

"Please send my condolences to her family." Alan picked up

a sheet of paper. "And now if you'll excuse me I have exams to grade."

"Your *daughter* ran away after the funeral," Jack said. "She's missing."

Alan shrugged. "I don't know where she is."

"We know that," Emily said.

"Her name is Alyson Walker." Jack's hand trembled as it reached into his breast pocket for a copy of the postcard. "Here's a picture of her."

Alan took it and studied it.

Alyson had her father's nose: long and narrow but straight and unobtrusive. That had to be the first thing Alan noticed.

It also looks just like yours.

"We were both at Whitmore then." Alan's forehead was creased. "How did she hide her pregnancy from me?"

"You remember Susan missing the first month of her junior year?" Emily sat straight in her chair, her feet flat on the floor.

Alan looked uncomfortable. He remembered.

"Having Alyson was the reason why." Emily raised her chin. "Fortunately, timing was on her side. She hardly showed her pregnancy for most of it, and by the time she did, it was summer break."

Alan put his hands behind his head. "So what are the chances of this girl's being found?"

"Excellent," Jack said, his voice firm and clear.

"How can you be so sure?"

He's hoping she stays missing.

"Jack's hired a private investigator," Emily said. "An ex-detective who specializes in missing persons."

"You want me to help pay for him? Is that what this is about?"

He glared at Jack, who was glaring at him.

You could be twins.

"This isn't about money, Alan." Emily sounded bored. "We'll take care of that. Alyson needs a parent. She's lost both her mothers, and her stepfather doesn't want to get involved. You're the only parent she has left."

"Now there's something I find interesting." Alan picked up the coffeepot from the credenza in back of him and filled his mug. "How come her stepfather wants nothing to do with her?"

"He divorced the woman who adopted Alyson eight years ago," Emily said.

"What kind of person is this girl?" Alan handed the photocopy back to Jack.

"You can keep that," Jack said.

"I don't want it."

Jack folded it back into fourths. The creases didn't line up. He unfolded it and folded it again. Emily and Alan were watching him.

"We've never met Alyson." Jack stuck the crooked photo back in his jacket. "But I bet she's special."

"So you don't know what kind of person she is?" Alan said it as if Jack hadn't done his homework. "She could be a criminal. She could be on drugs."

Get out of here!

No. They had to take this further.

Do it for Alyson.

"She's your daughter," Jack said, "your flesh and blood. She's missing. You have to care about that."

"Don't tell me what I should care about."

Jack made a fist.

Hit the bastard. Do it now. DO IT.

"Put yourself in my position, Jack." It was the first time Alan had called him by name. "As I said last night, Michelle and I don't want to be parents. I made that clear."

Jack shivered but he was sweating and his fist was still clenched. He looked at a mirror propped up against a pile of books on the desk and saw his own reflection. Sweat beaded his forehead. His shirt collar was damp. He shifted in his seat. It was a million degrees in here. The temperature didn't seem to be affecting Emily.

"You're already a parent," Jack said. "You have a responsibility. Don't you understand that?"

He imagined Alan Dean pinned against the wall. Jack throws a right. His knuckles collide with Dean's jaw. Blood flows from Dean's mouth. Jack screams, "You never loved Susan!" He throws a left. Dean stumbles. Jack screams louder, "You're NOT Alyson's father." Jack spits. *You would have been. But Susan and Alison died.* Jack keeps hitting Dean, harder and harder, a barrage of punches. Dean drops to the floor. Blood covers his face. His eyes are swollen. He wipes his mouth, looks up. The resemblance is still there.

Jack blinked. The images dissolved.

He looked out the window. It was summer break, but there were still students walking in the quadrangle. One girl sat cross-legged under a tree in the middle of it, reading. Two young men played Frisbee on either side of her.

"Alyson could be a student here." Jack pointed to the scene outside.

Alan jerked back like he'd been shot in the forehead but recovered almost immediately.

"Don't you think you're getting a little ahead of yourself?" He leaned forward and stared at Jack. Now Alan's image was in the mirror. "You haven't even found her and you're discussing her education. It's possible she's dead."

"She's alive!" Jack shouted. "ALIVE. You hear?"

"Why are you so sure?"

Jack opened his mouth. Nothing came out.

"What's wrong with you?" Alan asked.

Punch him NOW.

"It's okay with me, Jack," he heard Susan say.

"When Alyson disappeared she told a friend she didn't want

to wind up in a foster home," Emily said. "She might be looking for you."

"If she were, she'd have found me." Alan spread his arms. "I'm not hard to find. I'm in the phone book."

Jack said, "But she doesn't—"

Alan held up his hand.

"Let's assume this girl is alive and you do find her." His gaze moved toward the window. "It would be awkward if she attended Whitmore. I don't want her here. I want nothing to do with her." He turned toward them. "Maybe I should put it in writing. Would that help?"

"She's your daughter!" Jack yelled. "She's your DAUGHTER! When does that get through your thick skull?"

You'll regret not punching him.

"You're obsessive." Alan shook his head.

He knows you.

Jack shot up from his chair.

Emily held his arm. They looked at each other. Alan was watching them. Emily let go.

"You're heartless, Dean," Jack said. "I can't believe you exist."

Alan took off his reading glasses and folded them.

"We're all different, Jack, and Susan decided to keep this child from me. You should honor her wishes. It's best for everyone. After you calm down and think it over, you'll agree."

"Don't tell me to calm down, you pompous ass." Jack remade the fist.

"What are you going to do?" Alan stood up. "Hit me? Would that make you feel like a man? You really need to control yourself."

Jack, standing at the edge of the desk, turned to Emily.

"You're right, he IS a bastard."

"You're both sick." Alan crossed his arms.

"Screw you," Emily said.

"Get out." Alan pointed to the door.

They didn't move.

"Here's an idea." Alan leaned over the desk. "You think it's so easy? You two become Alyson's parents. Give it a try instead of shoving the responsibility onto me."

"You're not me," Jack said. "I'm not you."

"There's something we agree on. Now get out. And let's plan on never seeing each other's face again."

"You won't." Jack grabbed the mirror. He threw it at the floor, stomped on it, smashed it. Alan's eyebrows, nose, lips, eyes, all smithereens.

Nobody said anything.

Jack and Emily left.

CHAPTER 21

SUNLIGHT HIT THEM when they got outside, Jack's pulse racing as if he really had battered Alan Dean and not the mirror.

The young men were still playing Frisbee in the quadrangle.

You'll regret not hitting the son of a bitch.

The Frisbee flew over the head of the closest player and landed at Jack's feet. He picked it up and flung it into the bright blue sky. It landed in the furthest player's hand as if Jack had placed it there.

"You're good," Emily said as she shielded her eyes from the sun.

"That and trading is the extent of it."

Emily looked up at him, her green eyes blazing in the sunlight.

"I still want a scholarship in Susan's name. I just don't want it at Whitmore."

"We'll find someplace else. Someplace far from here." Jack watched a young couple walking together, holding hands. "Let's plan on never seeing Nestor again."

"I'm all for that." They resumed walking toward the parking lot. "The only thing I'll miss about Nestor is Eleanor. I like her. It was good to see her again."

Jack imagined Dean walking into Eleanor's bar and offering to buy Susan a drink.

"No!" he yelled.

"What?"

"Nothing. It's nothing."

"You want to tell me about it?" Emily asked.

Jack kept walking to the car. Emily waited outside while he started it. The leather seats were hot. He opened the windows and turned on the air conditioner. Moments later, Emily got in.

They left Whitmore's parking lot at noon.

"How could she have loved him?" Jack asked when they were back on the thruway. Waves of heat rose off the asphalt. Traffic was light. It wouldn't be later, when the weekend ended and everyone headed home.

"I'm sure Alan can be charming when he wants to be." Emily opened her window. She lit a cigarette. "Today we saw the real Alan Dean—the one that broke Susan's heart."

"Did she ever consider getting an abortion?" Jack asked.

"She went to a clinic but she couldn't go through with it. That's when she came to me."

"You were her sister. She knew she could trust you to keep her secret."

"It wasn't just that." She turned toward the window. "She knew I'd do anything to get closer to her."

"You're saying Susan used you?" He tightened his grip on the wheel. His heart beat faster.

"We used each other." Emily's voice sounded sad. "The truth is, I'm still trying to get close to her." She looked at him from the corner of her eye. "Pretty pathetic, huh?"

Emily finished her cigarette, closed the window, and reclined her seat. She fell asleep in a fetal position, hands clasped against her cheek.

Jack pulled into the right lane and set the cruise control for fifty-five.

Two hours later, he exited the thruway.

Emily opened her eyes, a little groggy. She looked good. She always did.

"I'll call you tomorrow," Jack said after he pulled into Emily's circular driveway. Her stone house looked like a castle.

"You okay with me helping you find Alyson?" Emily said.

"She's your niece."

"It has nothing to do with us doing something worthwhile together?" She raised her eyebrows.

Jack recalled the kiss he imagined they had.

"That too."

Emily looked at him and sighed. Why wasn't she getting out of the car?

"This is a good a time to make a confession," she said.

"And what might that be?"

"I had that postcard sent to you."

"You did what?" He was tired from the drive. He must have missed something.

"I got Alyson's postcard and had it sent to you."

"What are you talking about?" Blood rushed his face.

"I needed you to take charge."

Jack's brain twitched. He saw white. It was everywhere, pure and unadulterated white. His mind's eye was blank. No images. Not one. *Where are they?* He felt like he was falling, falling with nothing visual to grab hold of.

"You knew Alyson was missing before I did?" His voice shook.

"Yes." Emily looked down, her hair hid her eyes.

Jack grabbed the steering wheel, wishing it was Emily's neck.

"It was foolish. I shouldn't have deceived you." She caught hold of his arm. "Please forgive me."

Her words choked him. Her touch seared him.

He yanked his arm from her grasp, his elbow clipping her jaw in the process.

"Ow! You're scaring me, Jack."

"Get out."

"I wasn't trying to—"

"GET OUT!" He pounded the dashboard. His body was hot.

Fear was on her face. She reached for the door handle.

"DON'T YOU MOVE." He shook his head wildly. "Puppets—that's all people are to you, Emily, we're all just PUPPETS. Well, get this through your head–I am NOT your puppet!"

"I wasn't trying to hurt you!"

He stared straight ahead.

"Jack, please, look at me."

He didn't.

"Jack."

He closed his eyes. His muscles tightened. He clenched his teeth.

Emily stepped out of the car, pulled her suitcase from the backseat, and closed the door. Jack put the car in drive and took off.

CHAPTER 22

JACK WAS PARKED IN FRONT of a white brick condominium. It was 6:20 p.m. on Monday, the day after Emily hit him with her confession.

His cell vibrated, startling him. He flipped open the phone, checked the caller ID, and winced.

"Leave me alone!" he yelled as he stared out his front windshield. A young man walking a Chihuahua passed. The dog stopped and looked in Jack's direction. A tug on its leash forced it to continue on.

A minute passed. Jack's cell beeped. He blew out a breath. He had a message.

"Maybe he's calling to say don't call back," Jack said.

You should be so lucky.

Jack sighed and dialed his voicemail.

"Jack, please call me. We lost two more clients today." Sean's voice rose. "*I can't do this by myself* much longer."

Jack deleted the message and turned off his phone.

"Sorry partner, but I've got priorities and you're not one of them." He got out of his car, locked it, and looked up at the twenty-story building he was about to enter. "You're on your own, Sean. Just like me. And for the record, I'm scared witless."

Jack stepped into an elevator and pressed the button for the twentieth floor. The car was paneled in black marble, with thick gray carpeting on the floor. Jazz music played softly.

"Wait," a female voice shouted as the doors began to close. Jack pressed a button and they retreated.

"Thank you." The woman who stepped into the car looked to be in her sixties and reeked of Obsession. Jack named this character Hedda. Two miniature poodles trailed on either side of her—one white, one black, both perfectly groomed.

"Mind pushing the seventh floor?" Her voice trilled up at the end.

Jack pressed seven.

"Thank you." Her smile lingered as she fidgeted with the leashes.

The elevator began a quiet ascent.

The black dog sniffed Jack's shoe then mounted his leg. Jack fought the urge to shake him off and kick him.

"Buffy, please leave the nice man alone." Hedda pulled the dog's leash. Buffy obeyed after the third tug. "I'm so sorry. She's usually not like that." Hedda smiled. "She must like you."

Jack was sure Buffy had left some combination of dirt, saliva, and hair on his pants. The thought made him twitch, but he'd have to deal with that later.

Hedda looked toward the control panel. Her face darkened. "You're going to the twentieth floor?" she whispered.

Jack nodded.

Buffy mounted Jack's leg again.

Hedda yanked her away. Buffy sounded like she was choking.

A bell chimed and the elevator stopped. Hedda got off, head

down, pulling her poodles behind her. Buffy looked back at Jack and licked her chops.

The doors shut. They showed Jack's reflection. He wore a suit and tie, Reggie's suggestion.

Jack looked up and watched the floor numbers go higher. His pulse quickened. When the elevator came to a halt at twenty, his stomach hit the floor.

The doors parted.

He turned right and walked down a long hallway, came to a door, rang the bell. He heard footsteps.

The young man who came to the door was slender, with a mustache and short cropped hair. Jack named him Freddie.

"Mr. Logan?" he asked.

"Yes."

"Follow me."

It was cold inside the apartment. The air conditioning must've been on high. Along the hallway, spotlights shone on framed movie posters. One showed a buxom blonde in a bikini with a machine-gun leg. Another showed six men in suits and sunglasses with pistols drawn.

"Mr. Walker's on a conference call," Freddie said as they walked into a spacious living room. Dusk was settling in. "He'll be with you shortly." He brightened the track lighting and left.

When Reggie called Alyson's stepfather to set up a meeting, John Walker had said he told the police everything he knew and saw no reason to meet. Reggie pressed him, telling him who his client was. John said he'd meet with Jack—alone.

Now Jack was sitting on a big thick couch. Its pillows had spearhead designs befitting the room's southwestern decor: area rugs on a terracotta floor, a tall cactus in one corner, a colorful woven basket in the other. Turquoise vases lined the mantel of the huge fireplace. A cast iron kettle was next to it and a sun-bleached steer skull rested on the oversized carved wood coffee table.

Jack ran his finger along the skull. It was smooth. He pictured the animal it had once belonged to, grazing in a field, unsuspecting.

"I found that in Taos." John Walker stood in the doorway. He was short and round with a pencil-thin mustache. "What do you think of it?"

"It's interesting."

"Come on, Mr. Logan, I won't be offended if you don't like it."

"It depresses me."

"A maudlin response, but better." John pulled in a deep breath. "It makes me feel alive."

Alyson's stepfather walked with a forearm crutch, his left hip clearly the culprit.

Jack's eyes lingered on it.

"A car accident six years ago," John said. "She was drunk and drifted into the left lane of I-90. I ran into the back of her."

"Sorry to hear that."

"Don't be. I married her. And whatever doesn't kill you really does make you stronger." John made his way over to the bay window across from the entrance. "But you're not here to find out how I met my wife or discuss my philosophy of life." He looked at his watch. "And I have a conference call in fifteen minutes, Mr. Logan, so ask me what you must."

"When was the last time you saw Alyson?"

John gave him a hard look. "You sound like a detective and I'm a suspect."

"I'm just trying to find her." Jack looked at the steer skull. "What is wrong with you people?"

"Huh?" John raised his crutch.

You fool. You're screwing this up.

"Sorry…it's just that this has been a bit frustrating." Jack unbuttoned his jacket and buttoned it again.

A bit frustrating? It's driving you nuts.

"I haven't seen Alyson since my divorce. That was in ninety-nine."

The first person you've met who's met Alyson.

Jack shivered. "Alyson has your last name. You weren't close to her?"

"You're looking in the wrong place." John leaned against the window sill. "Alyson and I were never close."

"Still, she's missing."

Is he another Alan Dean? They're all over the place.

"I've cooperated with the police. They believe she's a runaway. Mary had plenty of money, I saw to that. Alyson is rich. Now if you'll excuse me, Mr. Logan, I have to make some of that money back."

"Please, just take a look at this." Jack unfolded a photocopy of the postcard and handed it to John. Reggie had said to watch John's reaction.

"The police showed me this." John was looking at the picture. "This is a waste of time."

If Alyson's stepfather felt anything, he didn't show it.

"Can you think of any logical place she'd go?" Jack asked.

"Alyson kept to herself. She mostly played with her Barbie dolls." John appeared to have a bitter taste in his mouth. "She was like her mother. She liked to stay home. Running away was out of character for the girl I knew."

"If this were a movie what would you have her do?"

"Mr. Logan, have you seen any of my movies?" John handed the picture back to Jack. "Now, I have a—"

"Dad, you ready? We've got another call in ten minutes and we need to discuss the screenplay first."

Jack looked up and saw a man in his twenties in the doorway. He was tall, lanky, and so handsome it was hard to look at him.

He bopped over towards them.

"Mr. Logan, this is my stepson, Roman." John was beaming. "He's directing our current project."

"I may be the screenwriter, too, if we can't find someone who writes decent dialogue." He looked at Jack with a cocked eyebrow. "You write?"

This could be your chance.

"No," John said, "but we'll find another writer by the end of the week."

"Roman Dedalus." He shook Jack's hand.

Jack took back the picture of Alyson.

"What's that?" Roman pointed to the picture.

Jack handed it to him.

"It's not what you think," John eyed Jack. "In fact, Mr. Logan was just leaving. Isn't that right?"

"Ha!" Roman flicked the picture with his finger. "She already auditioned for me three months ago." He looked at his stepfather. "She's Alyson Tierney, the cocktail waitress."

Alyson was an actress? Susan had been in a local theater group, but she let go of her dream after they got engaged.

You saw to that.

"She's the one working at the Rendezvous?" John looked incredulous.

Jack's heart raced.

Roman nodded. "That's the one."

"What's the Rendezvous?" Jack asked.

"Topless bar on the East Side," Roman said. "We're shooting the bar scenes there."

"Alyson's a cocktail waitress at a topless bar." Jack held his head.

"Best way to prepare her for the part," Roman said. "Detail, I'm into detail."

"There must be some mistake." Jack took his hands off his head and looked from Roman to John and back. "Alyson's fifteen years old."

"She proved she was twenty-one."

"It had to be fake ID."

"What agency are you from?" Roman asked.

"He's not a talent agent," John said. "He's looking for that girl." His face reddened as he pointed to the picture. "She's my ex-wife's daughter."

"The Recluse Wife?"

John nodded. "You're sure she's still working there?"

"Spoke to her last week. She's really fifteen?"

"Yes," John and Jack said at the same time.

"Damn, I liked her." Roman pulled in a deep breath, looked around. "Time for damage control."

"What do we do?" Jack was shaking. He wished Reggie was there. Hell, he'd even take Emily.

"I don't know about you, but I'm calling Mickey." Roman removed a red business card from his wallet and picked up the phone.

"Who's Mickey?" Jack asked.

"The owner of the Rendezvous," John said.

"She's there now?" Jack couldn't imagine this.

"She starts at eight." Roman was already pushing buttons, "same time as in the movie."

Jack looked at his watch. "It's a quarter to seven." He grabbed the handset from Roman.

"What are you doing?"

"Give me until nine," Jack said without thinking.

You need to get there by eight.

"And I should do this because?" Roman said.

"I need to talk to her."

"Do it after they fire her. Now give me my phone."

"She might disappear before I can," Jack said. "Please, I need some time."

"That's not my problem." Roman took the handset from Jack.

Adrenaline sped through Jack's veins. He looked around, his mind searching for options. He could grab John and hold him hostage. Ridiculous. He eyed the business card Roman held between two fingers.

Take it and run.

"Wait." John looked at Roman. "Maybe there's an opportunity here. Let's give Mr. Logan what he asked for."

"How does that help us?" Roman asked.

"He can get her to quit and Mickey won't find out she's a minor. Then our only problem will be finding another cocktail waitress and not another topless bar." John looked at Jack. "You willing to do this?"

You have to.

"Give me until nine."

"Good," John said.

"I don't like this, Dad."

"Trust me, this is the best way. She won't make a scene."

"What's the address?" Jack asked.

"Take this." Roman handed the business card to Jack.

Jack ran his finger over the raised gold lettering.

You need help.

"Make sure you tell her she just derailed her acting career," Roman said as Jack ran out the door.

CHAPTER 23

JACK ACCELERATED ONTO the parkway. He was heading south, towards the city, taking the same route Susan would have taken the day she and Alison died. He hadn't driven to the city since that day.

His eyes were burning. It was hard to see.

The Rendezvous was in midtown. Its business card claimed it was a gentleman's club. Jack did a double-take after he read its address.

It's the same block?

He'd know for sure if he saw Way-Lo Electronics on the corner. The truck Susan ran into had been double-parked there.

That's assuming you make it.

He'd called Reggie as soon as he left John Walker's. It went straight to voicemail. Jack left a message telling the PI what he found out and where he was headed. He'd wanted to do this alone. Now he wasn't so sure. His chance for redemption and he wasn't ready for it.

He pushed a button and his car's sunroof slid back, letting in more of the fading daylight. Clouds moved towards him. They were big and dark and looked ready to burst. He opened the windows and listened to his tires slap the road. His foot pressed the accelerator and his car breezed ahead, cutting through thick air, cutting through twilight.

The parkway spread to three lanes. When he saw the sign for the expressway, he bore right and merged onto it. Minutes later, he came to an amber bridge. It looked rusty. His tires whined as they made their way over its grooved metal pavement.

"I hate this bridge." Susan had said that every time they went over it. She would've had to drive over it that day. He wanted to floor the gas and smash into one of the bridge's steel beams, putting an end to his misery. But that would be just another selfish act.

You're damned if you live, damned if you die.

Jack didn't bother to check over his shoulder as he crossed the two lanes on his right. A horn beeped. "Shove it!" He got onto the entrance ramp for the East River Drive. It was crawling. He merged onto it, eventually. Lights flashed in the distance.

"Someone's screwing up my life again," Jack yelled at the windshield. "Why do you people always do it at the worst times?"

It was 7:35 p.m. He was still a good twenty minutes from Alyson.

Jack's foot danced between the brake and the accelerator until he reached the First Avenue exit. He got off and headed west.

Skyscrapers towered on either side of him.

"They're about to fall," Susan said.

Jack checked the passenger seat and there she was, looking up at the buildings with her mouth open and anguished eyes. He was mesmerized.

A kid on a scooter shot out in front of the car. Jack screeched to a halt, barely missing him. The car sat there, panting. Jack shoved the shift to park.

Get out of the car, Logan. RUN.

"Look." Susan pointed to a teenage girl on the corner. The girl had on fishnet stockings, stiletto heels, and a black leather miniskirt. She had short dirty blond hair and too much eyeliner. Her pink shirt, torn on the shoulder, said *Bitch* in sparkling script across the front. "You can't let Alyson wind up like that," Susan said. "Do something, Jack."

All around him, horns blared. "Hey, jackass, move!" from the cabdriver behind him. "Come on!" from another voice in the distance.

You're pissing people off.

"Hon, you've got to leave," Jack said. "I need to focus."

Jack felt her kiss his cheek. Then she was gone. Now the horns were deafening.

"I love you." Jack put his car in drive. "Always have, always will."

He turned onto Sixtieth Street and saw the blue neon sign for the Rendezvous on his right. Rain started falling on his head. He closed his sunroof and turned his wipers on low. He went past the Rendezvous, surveying the area.

A stoplight was up ahead.

Way-Lo Electronics was on the corner.

His heart beat faster. The loading zone in front of the store was empty. Had it been empty the day Susan died, she'd still be alive. He held his breath.

The rain came down harder. Steady.

Jack tightened his grip on the wheel.

The light turned red. He had to stop in front of the store.

Rain pelted his car.

After an eternity, the light turned green. Now he could leave the spot where he'd lost what mattered most in his life. But he couldn't move. Not just yet.

It was 7:55.

You've got to get going.

The light turned yellow. He sped through the intersection.

The quick getaway caused him to miss his turn. The next block was one way going the wrong way. He made a right at the block after that and drove past the building where the best obstetrician in the state had his first floor office. The article that said so was framed in his waiting room. They should've stopped going there after the first visit.

But you couldn't give in.

Jack made another right and headed back to the Rendezvous, Gunn's building behind him.

Susan was so close.

Jack had assumed the pressure of the drive had taken control of her emotions and caused the accident. Now he sensed it was something else. It was out there, daring him to find it.

Careful what you wish for.

The rain eased as he pulled in front of the topless bar and a young man in dress pants and sneakers stepped up to his window.

"How long will you be?"

"An hour." Jack left the door open and the motor running. He put a five in the valet's palm and headed toward the entrance, sidestepping puddles along the way.

CHAPTER 24

THE FIRST THING JACK SAW when he walked into the Rendezvous was a big man in a dark suit. The man's eyes moved toward a sign that stated the cover charge. Jack gave him a twenty and proceeded down a wide hallway with pictures of nearly naked women framed on either side. At the end of the hall, he was hit by an orgy of music and light. Then he turned into a huge room with a platform stage.

The bar that wrapped the stage was surrounded by men, most of them middle-aged. Some had thinning hair or pot bellies, some were good looking, some were talking to young women in high heels and short silk robes. Everyone was drinking. Everyone seemed to be having a good time.

He looked around and didn't see Alyson. It was 8:15.

She should've started by now.

Jack had never been to a topless bar before. He ran a finger between his neck and shirt collar. Adrenaline sped through his veins.

On the stage, a red velvet chair sat between two gold poles. A young woman was climbing a ladder that led onto the stage. She was wearing spike heels and a G-string. She had a pretty face, long gold hair, and a beautiful figure.

"Please welcome Tara." A deep voice boomed from the loudspeakers.

A song he never heard before played while red, white, and blue lights caressed Tara's body. She danced slowly, her arms wrapped around herself, legs busy.

Small round tables were scattered around the room. Rows of high-back booths lined the walls. Most of the tables were for two and most were empty. But it was still early on a Monday night.

Tara raised her fists above her head and pumped her pelvis at the men looking up at her. Drums pounded the speakers. Bass thumped the floor. She whipped her head in circles, hair slapping her face as she puckered her lips.

Jack found an empty table away from the stage. It was dark there. He looked left and saw a middle-aged man and a young woman sitting next to each other in a high-back booth. The man was wearing a suit. The woman's robe was open. She had one of her legs slung over his. She was young enough to be his daughter.

Jack wanted to move so he wouldn't have to watch this scene unfold. But he didn't want to be conspicuous. So he stayed, eyes roaming the room, searching for Alyson.

Blue lights shone on the spaces between the tables. The air was cool and thin. Traces of sweet perfume snuck up on him.

Tara stopped and squatted as a businessman slid a bill under her G-string. Soon a bunch of bills were sticking out of it. She shook her shoulders and smiled flirtatiously as she danced to the other side of the bar.

Jack turned away—and saw Alyson serving drinks to the man and the woman in the booth. Jack shifted in his seat, his fingertips trembling.

Alyson was twenty feet away.

He blinked.

She was still there.

Susan's daughter had shoulder-length blond hair. She was wearing high heels and a sequined white dress. It was tight, short, and low-cut.

Jack found her alluring. The sensation disturbed him.

She doesn't look fifteen.

He shuddered as he watched her talk to the man in the booth.

Alyson smiled and laughed as if she knew him.

The man said something in Alyson's ear, his hand needlessly on her shoulder.

Jack made a fist.

The man finished talking. He reached inside his jacket. Alyson shook her head, polite but firm. She showed him her palm and said something.

The man held up his hands—feigning innocence. Alyson turned away from the booth, shaking her head as she made her way towards Jack.

Jack's stomach churned acid.

She looks just like Susan.

"Hi, I'm Candace." Alyson put her foot on the rung of the chair opposite Jack. "What can I get you?" She slid a bowl of nuts onto the table and held a tray against her hip, a smile lingering on her face.

Candace?

He looked around the room. These women probably used stage names.

Candace must be the character in Roman's movie.

"I'll have a vodka tonic, please," Jack said.

"Be right back." Alyson turned on her heels and walked towards the bar.

Jack looked to his right. A huge dark-skinned man wearing

sunglasses stood in the corner. He scanned the room, his head bobbing to the beat of the music. His eyes settled on Jack.

Why?

Without thinking, Jack popped two nuts into his mouth. They tasted salty and made him thirsty. He recalled reading an article that said bar-room nuts contained twenty-seven types of urine. He wanted to spit them out.

Too late.

He looked up. Alyson was walking back toward him with his drink. He knew exactly what he'd say, just not when he'd say it. That moment came after he gave her a tip.

"Hello, Alyson."

She looked at him quizzically.

He took the postcard from his inside breast pocket and handed it to her.

Sunglasses saw this and scowled. He didn't move, but he was watching.

You better be careful.

Alyson picked up the postcard and shook her head.

"Not me." She tossed the postcard on the table. It landed next to the nuts.

"We both know it is." Jack stirred his drink, trying to appear relaxed. Sweat seeped from his pores.

"You see that man wearing sunglasses? In the corner near the door? I call him over and you're out of here."

"You won't do that." He held her stare.

She's beautiful.

"You think so?" She had her tray against her chest.

"I've got more to tell you."

"Are you a cop?"

"I'm…a friend."

She looked at his cuffs.

"My name is Jack. Jack Logan."

"I don't know you."

"They're about to find out your real age." Jack looked toward the bar as if "they" were there. Alyson played her part well, though he suspected her heart was racing as fast as his. "Roman's going to tell them at nine."

"No one here's named Roman."

"I'm trying to help you." Jack squeezed his glass. "There isn't much time."

"I don't need help…yours or anyone else's." A young man took a seat two tables away. Alyson looked at him and said, "I've got to go."

"Roman saw this picture of you." Jack pointed to the post-card as she turned away. "So did your stepfather."

She stopped.

"You ever hear of Susan Logan?" That was a slip. If Mary Walker had told Alyson about her birth mother she wouldn't have known Susan's married name. "I meant White, Susan White. You ever hear of her?"

"I've heard of Susan Logan." Alyson was looking at the floor.

"Your mother told you?"

It took a minute, but Alyson looked up at him.

"Susan Logan died on this street three months ago." Alyson spoke slowly, then pointed as if in a trance. "It was in front of the electronics store."

Alyson knew about the accident?

The room was spinning. Jack wanted to sip his drink but couldn't lift the glass. He couldn't get a grip on it. Everything was out of place, out of focus. He couldn't breathe. The music was too loud. His head pounded, about to explode. He grabbed the sides of the table and held on tight.

Alyson looked up. Pain was etched on her face.

"Why are you asking me about Susan Logan?"

Sunglasses was moving towards them, taking his time. Probably so he wouldn't draw attention. He was approaching from behind Alyson.

"Susan Logan was my wife." Jack closed his eyes, a finger on each eyelid, trying to use the last moments he had to find the strength to tell Alyson that Susan Logan was also her mother.

When he opened his eyes, Alyson was gone.

CHAPTER 25

JACK KNOCKED OVER A CHAIR as he ran toward the entrance of the Rendezvous.

Sunglasses blocked his path, his arms crossed.

"What'd you say to that girl?"

"I told her to go back to college." Jack met his stare. The man had to be at least six inches taller than him. "Now get out of my way."

"What, you trying to save the world?" Sunglasses stepped closer, bumped Jack's chest.

"Just that girl. Now let me go."

"Men don't come here to save." Sunglasses had onions on his breath. "They come to be saved." He pointed to the door. "Get out and don't come back."

Jack ran past him.

"Walk!" Sunglasses shouted. Jack ignored him.

It was pouring outside. Jack was in the middle of the street, getting soaked. Muffled music came from the Rendezvous.

Two girls sharing an umbrella passed. The valet was leaning against a car, wearing a poncho.

Offer him a hundred for that poncho.

"You see where she went?" Jack asked.

"You mean the waitress?"

"Yes. Alyson. Damn. I mean Candace."

"She went that way." The valet pointed.

Jack turned and ran. Running felt good. He went faster. Rain hit his face and his shoes thumped the pavement. "Bastard," an old man muttered after Jack bumped into him. "Idiot!" a woman shouted when a puddle Jack landed in splashed her.

"Sorry!" he called over his shoulder.

At the end of the block Jack looked both ways, crossed the street, and kept going. Most stores were closed. Streetlights sprayed soft light. A man and a woman were standing under an awning in front of a bodega.

"You see a girl run past here?" Jack slowed to ask them.

"You want this one?" The man shoved his head toward the woman. Her eyes were lifeless as she flicked her cigarette.

Jack heard footsteps. They sounded like high heels. He sped up and went right.

He saw a figure, walking quickly, wearing a hooded white raincoat. He wiped his eyes and blinked.

It's her.

"Alyson!" he yelled.

She went left, running fast.

Now apartment buildings were on either side of him. Alyson couldn't be far. It was dark. He smelled urine. He sidestepped a pile of steaming feces. A black cat meowed and brushed his ankle. Jack's lungs were burning and his legs ached. He kept running, pushing himself. He was close, but where was Alyson?

Panting, he looked around at the buildings.

A red door was on his left. He pulled its handle. It didn't budge. He pulled harder. No use. A black door was next to it.

It was locked too. He pounded. Listened. Silence. He pounded the door again. More silence. No one.

He cupped his hands around his mouth.

"ALYSON!" he shouted at the sky as the rain drowned out his voice. He kept calling her name until he couldn't anymore.

You lost her.

Exhausted, he fell to his knees, closed his eyes, and prayed.

When he opened his eyes he saw Alyson, pausing to catch her breath in the soft haze of a streetlight.

"Thank you." He glanced at the sky.

Alyson ran. Jack took off after her.

"PLEASE, wait!"

She disappeared. At the end of the alley he stopped, looked left then right. He heard footsteps and ran across the street. A horn blared as a car screeched to a halt. Jack pushed off its hood.

"Idiot!" its driver yelled.

Jack kept running. He came to a white door and turned its rusty knob. Inside was a vestibule with a fluorescent ceiling light, buzzing. Up three steps was a black door. He yanked its handle. The door opened so suddenly he fell backwards. He got up and went inside, jogged up one flight of stairs, then another. *Get to the roof.* On the fourth floor a door was ajar. He held his breath and pushed it. He stepped inside. It was dark, but he found a wall and felt his way toward a light up ahead. His eyes adjusted to the darkness. He kept moving. He came to a group of female mannequins. Some were missing arms. All were naked.

She's not here.

He ran out of the room. He climbed one level and came to a door with an *A* on it. *That's it.* He rammed his shoulder against the door. He went inside, looked down, and found a trapdoor. He opened that and found a set of stairs. He trotted down them. Another door. This one had an *L*.

Jack scratched his head. He found a revolving door, spinning. He stepped through that and came to a door with an *I* on it. He tripped over a mannequin's arm. He was falling, tumbling down, seeing stars. THUD. He landed flat on his back.

Jack opened his eyes. He was outside. It was still raining. He ran out of the alley. His legs reached out, arms pumping, lungs gasping for air. At Twenty-third Street he hopped a cab back to the Rendezvous. He got his car and drove home, his mind now a blank.

"If it wasn't for that bouncer..." Jack stopped rocking and leaned forward, elbows on his knees. "I'd have caught up to her."

Jack and Reggie were sitting in two oak rocking chairs on Jack's front porch. Rain pelted the slate roof above them. It hadn't stopped since yesterday, it just eased occasionally then picked up again.

"You had quite the night." Reggie's eyes were sympathetic, each iris a kaleidoscope of brown, taupe, tan.

Jack pointed to the ceiling. "This rain didn't help."

"Jack, we've been through this a dozen times. You did your best. Sometimes stuff happens. Face it and move on."

Jack sneezed and felt a lump at the back of his throat, which often preceded a cold. He kept swallowing, hoping it would go away. It didn't.

"I checked out the address they had on file for Alyson at the Rendezvous." Reggie's small spiral-bound notebook lay open on one of his muscular thighs. He had on leather sandals, white shorts, and a red knit polo shirt. It was the first time Jack hadn't seen him in a suit. "The landlord said she moved out last night. She didn't leave a forwarding address." He shut his notebook. "No surprise there."

"You should've seen Alyson's reaction after I said Susan's name." Jack went back to that moment at the Rendezvous. "Something took control of her, something she couldn't hide."

"Sure you're not reading too much into this?" Reggie examined his fingernails.

"I'm sure. There's more to the story." He remembered the question he'd been meaning to ask. "Do you know when Alyson started working at the Rendezvous?"

Reggie flipped through his notebook, stopped, and flicked a page.

"April eleventh."

"That doesn't fit." Now Jack was standing. "Susan's accident was on the second. Why was Alyson there?"

Reggie shrugged.

"We're missing something." Jack looked at the floor as if the answer were there.

"We need more facts, simple as that." Reggie stood up. "Speculating like this is a waste of time."

The sky was slate gray. The air was thick enough to grab and at times it smelled rancid. Before yesterday there had been a string of hot sunny days. Now they were gone.

"I've got something to show you." Jack headed into the house. "It's in the attic, I'll be right back."

Three minutes later, Jack was back on the porch.

"Last week I found this letter Susan wrote to Alyson." He handed it to Reggie. "She never mailed it."

Reggie unfolded the letter.

"At first I didn't know it was to Alyson," Jack said. "I thought it was a love letter."

Reggie began reading. A cool breeze raised the hair on Jack's arms. Despite the roof above them, the wind pushed the rain in through the sides. Lightning streaked the sky. Thunder rumbled. A dog was barking. Reggie finished the letter, his eyes distant as he folded it and handed it back.

Jack slipped the letter into the envelope and put it inside Susan's favorite book, *Living Happy*.

"I see why you thought it was a love letter," Reggie said. "Another example of how things often aren't what they seem. It's why you always need the facts."

"I didn't trust Susan. How could I have done that?"

"I made the same mistake once, only I chose not to give her a chance to explain. You didn't have that opportunity."

You didn't let Emily explain.

"What do we do next?" Jack asked.

"I think someone's helping Alyson, and I think it could be Nolan Chance—the son of the neighbor who reported her missing."

"Alyson seems like a loner to me. You really think she has someone helping her?"

"Even a loner needs someone they can trust." Reggie wagged his finger between them. "We know that."

"What about going back to the Rendezvous?" Jack said. "Alyson has worked there for three months. Someone there must know something about her."

"I'll go to the Rendezvous." Reggie nodded at Jack. "You talk to the Chances."

"But I've already been to the Rendezvous."

"You don't know who you're dealing with in those places. Hell, in that whole neighborhood."

He doesn't know the half of it.

"Especially when you start asking questions about a minor." Reggie slipped his hands into his pockets. "I'll handle the Rendezvous."

"I know the place, Reggie. Let me go."

"You won't get past the bouncer."

"I'll wear glasses, part my hair, I can even—"

"You got to be kidding me," Reggie said.

"If Nolan's helping her, why would he tell the police Alyson ran away?"

"A runaway doesn't draw as much attention as someone who's been abducted." Reggie started pacing.

Jack saw himself sitting in the Chance's living room, sipping the ice tea Mrs. Chance would surely offer him while Nolan sat on the couch between his parents.

He looked up just as Emily's red Volvo pulled into his driveway next to Reggie's big black Buick. His heart raced.

"That Susan's sister?" Reggie asked, following Jack's gaze.

He nodded.

"I'm leaving." Reggie wrote something on a sheet in his notebook, tore it out, and handed it to him. "Here's the Chances' address. I'll call you at eight. You got this under control?"

"Sure," he said, not sure if Reggie meant the Chances or Emily.

CHAPTER 26

"SO THAT'S REGGIE." Emily was standing on the porch eyeing Jack, the wind playing with her hair. She pushed strands of it away from her face.

Jack crossed his arms against his chest, steeling himself, trying not to give in to the feeling that he was glad to see her. His body felt light, his heart thumped as pleasure and anger vied for position inside him.

Which one wins?

Emily sat in the rocking chair Reggie had used and pulled her low-cut silky black dress over her knees. She'd once said black was her power color.

No argument there.

Jack sat on the edge of the chair next to her.

"Is there anything new about Alyson?" Emily's voice was firm. He sensed she was giving whatever they had a chance but he'd have to meet her halfway.

"You've got a hell of a nerve coming here and acting like you did nothing wrong," Jack said.

She looked down. "I was hoping you've forgiven me by now."

"Not that easy."

"Do you really think I was trying to hurt you?" She slipped out of her open-toe pumps and rested her bare heels on the bottom rung of the chair.

"You should've been honest with me from the beginning." He leaned over the arm of his chair towards her, his body hot.

"You're right." She raised her chin. "I'm sorry."

"Why didn't you just ask me to help you?" Jack stood and started pacing, trying to control his emotions. It wasn't easy.

"That was my first option."

"But you didn't choose it."

"I thought about it—maybe too much. In the end, I did what I thought was best for me…and you."

He stopped pacing and glared at her. "Oh, so you did this for my benefit too?"

"I wanted you to take charge, but I didn't want to spring it on you all at once." Emily held her knees against her chest. "That's why I had that postcard sent to you."

"Take charge? Why?" He spread his arms. "Give me the logic, please."

"I couldn't do it alone." She produced a cigarette and lit it.

"Cut the crap. Let me say it again, why didn't you just ask me?" He watched smoke curl out of her mouth.

"How would you have reacted?"

How WOULD you?

Jack saw himself in his living room, sitting in the dark, slowly losing his grip on reality. The phone rings. He doesn't move. The answering machine comes on. It's Emily. *Damn.* He picks up. She tells him Susan has a daughter, she's missing, and Emily needs him to take charge finding her.

What?

When the first postcard came, he shredded it. He kept the second. Still didn't act on it. It wasn't until two days later when he saw Alyson on the milk carton and on TV that he committed. After that he found out who she really was. It was a gradual process. Looking back on it, he was grateful for that. He was in a bad place and needed time to process all the twists. He was still angry, still hurt. Still wished Emily had been honest with him up front. But maybe there was some sense to her logic. Maybe she knew him better than he thought. Jack felt unsteady. He sat back down.

"You put those postcards in my mailbox?" He couldn't picture her doing that. She was above that.

Wasn't she?

"I had the company that distributes them mail the cards to your zip code. I'd worked with them before on some real estate distributions. It was a five-minute phone call."

Rain was still coming down. Wind still blowing. The storm had intensified just when it seemed like it couldn't anymore. They were in the middle of the porch—the best spot if you had to be outside during a storm. He considered inviting her in but decided against it.

"Is there anything else you need to tell me?" Jack asked. "Let's get it all out in the open once and for all."

Emily nodded, took a breath and let it out slowly.

"I want to adopt her, Jack."

"You mean like be her guardian?"

"What else would I be?"

A very bad influence on her.

"You're serious." He felt like he'd been hit with a sledgehammer.

"It'll be good for me and Alyson." Emily placed her cigarette in the ashtray.

"Emily. You're an amazing woman, intelligent, resourceful, but you're not parent material."

"Thanks, Jack." Her eyes hardened.

He imagined Alyson's twenty-first birthday. She and Emily

sitting in a bar, smoking cigarettes and drinking dirty martinis. They clink glasses after hatching a plan to manipulate their next victim. Maybe him. This would be worse than Alyson winding up with Dean.

You HAVE to change Emily's mind.

He needed a plan. He had to take action. Words were useless against Emily. He'd do something drastic if that's what it took.

You can't kill her.

And yet she was the one killing his chance for redemption. Alyson would be better off if he didn't find her than if Emily adopted her.

"What do I do?" he yelled.

"Do about what?" Emily looked perplexed.

Give her a million, two if that's what it takes. You must protect Alyson. Do what you have to.

He shook his head wildly.

"For now, let's focus on finding Alyson." He stood up. "Which, by the way, I did last night."

"You found her?"

He hadn't planned to tell her yet. The words just snuck out of his mouth. He wasn't as good at keeping things from her as she was from him.

That could become a problem.

Emily grabbed his arms. "Where is she? When can I see her?"

"She slipped away." He stepped back.

"But you talked to her."

"I did."

Jack pictured Alyson boarding a plane. John Walker had said she had money. If she wanted to be an actress she might go to Hollywood. He'd run that possibility by Reggie.

"Come on, Jack, don't hold out on me. Alyson and I need each other." Emily picked up her cigarette and tapped it. Ash was whisked away on a breeze. "I need to care about someone. She needs someone to care about her. It makes perfect sense."

"Nothing you do makes perfect sense."

The same could be said about you.

"I'm serious." Now Emily started pacing, her arms flailing. "I could never get close to Susan. My love life is a joke. I need someone who needs me. That's Alyson."

"When did this come about? This decision."

You fool. She's been deceiving you all along.

"It happened in Dean's office. I had to after that."

"We shouldn't be talking about this now." Jack shoved his hands in his pockets to hide his trembling fingers.

You NEED to talk her out of this. Bad for Alyson. Bad for your redemption.

"When should we?" Emily looked around. "I bet she's close by. Someone has to be her guardian. Who's that going to be?"

He shrugged.

There was a beat.

"I'll never deceive you again," Emily said.

"You'll get another one of your wild ideas and you won't be able to stop yourself. You're manipulative, Emily. That's a fact."

"When you're lonely it's easy to fall into that trap."

"Maybe you're lonely because of the things you do."

"Maybe it's the other way around." Emily looked defiant. Or cornered.

"I'll think about that."

"I want us to be friends." She stubbed out her cigarette. "It's strange, your being Susan's husband, but I can't deny my feelings." Emily raised an eyebrow. "So are we? Friends?" She stuck out her hand.

He held it. It was soft yet firm. He didn't want to let go.

Since their lunch at Daniela's, he'd sensed there was something between them. Something he now knew Emily felt too. They both knew ignoring it wouldn't make it go away. There was the Emily he could love, the Emily he never wanted to see again, and the Emily who'd always be his wife's half-sister. Confusion was his only certainty.

"Friends," he said and let go of her hand.

He told her what had happened at John Walker's apartment, at the Rendezvous, and what he and Reggie planned to do next.

"Now I've got to go to the Chances," he said. "Would you like to come?" He'd forgiven her sooner than he thought he would.

That could be another problem.

"I think it's better if you go alone." She smiled. "The two of us together might intimidate them." She straightened her dress and stepped into her pumps.

There's something about her.

"I want to take care of her, Jack." Emily held his arms. His heart fluttered. "It'll be good for me…and Alyson." She looked up at him.

"We'll talk about that later."

You WILL stop her.

"Thank you." She kissed one cheek, held the other. "Good luck at the Chances. Call me when you can." She turned and ran through the rain to her car.

CHAPTER 27

JACK WATCHED EMILY back her red Volvo out of his driveway. It came to an abrupt halt when it was parallel to the house.
He pictured her emerging from it, running towards him, and
winding up in his arms. He closed his eyes, imagining how
she'd feel, the scent of her hair, the things they'd tell each other,
and what they would do when they stopped talking. But when
he opened his eyes, he saw the Volvo disappear around the
corner, leaving him disappointed.

And relieved.

He shut the front door behind him. Up in his bedroom, he
removed his gray tweed jacket from a hanger and laid it on the
bed. The navy blazer he'd worn last night at the Rendezvous was
still damp. Alyson might go back there, maybe even tonight.

You should've looked for her on your own.

Twenty minutes later Jack had on black slacks, a white shirt,
red tie, and the gray jacket. He checked himself in the mirror
above his dresser and remembered going to Alice Walker's

house, sweating, overwhelmed by the task in front of him. Now he was calmer.

But you haven't changed.

He straightened his tie, turned off his bedroom light, and headed down to the garage.

Ridgewood was a half-hour away. If he got there by five-thirty, odds were that at least one Chance, if not all three, would be home. The neighborhood was upper middle class— a step above where Alyson and the Chances used to live. Maybe they'd moved because Mr. Chance was promoted. Or was their reason for moving somehow related to Alyson's disappearance?

Jack was about to push the button to open the garage when the doorbell rang. It hadn't rung much the past three months. It sounded strange, especially at that hour.

Emily?

He walked down the hallway that led to the front door, his mind racing through possibilities. None were good. When the bell rang twice in succession, he shuddered.

Could she have been in an accident?

Sensations from the day he lost Susan and Alison swept over him. He held his breath, reached for the doorknob, and turned it. He hoped this wouldn't be a moment he'd never forget.

Sean was standing there—in the sunlight. It had stopped raining.

"Catch you at a bad time?" He was swaying.

"I'm on my way to meet someone."

"I won't take long." Sean looked on either side of him. "I won't even ask to come in."

"You've got five minutes." Jack stepped out onto the porch, closed the front door behind him, and locked it.

His partner needed a shave. His hair needed combing, his eyes were bloodshot, and his breath smelled of alcohol. He had on chinos, canvas topsiders, and a light windbreaker with half of his shirt collar sticking out. He looked younger than thirty-two.

"You get my messages?" Sean rubbed the stubble on his chin. Jack nodded.

"Why didn't you call me back?"

"I'm busy." Jack tapped his foot, the hairs on the back of his neck erect.

"He's looking for that missing girl," Sean said over his shoulder as if someone were behind him. "I'm at my wit's end and he's out playing detective."

"I don't have to account for my time." Jack's eyelid twitched. "Especially to you."

"I'm your partner," Sean said. "You can't just bail on me."

"I thought work was keeping you sane?"

"It was." Sean pulled a pint bottle of vodka from under his windbreaker. "Now this is." He took a long pull on it, then held it up towards Jack.

"No thanks."

"Come on, Jackie, a little drink with your partner for old times' sake." He shook the open bottle. The vodka sloshed back and forth, sending a wave of nausea through Jack.

"You drove here like this?" he said.

"I took a cab. Now you'll have a drink?"

"I said no."

"Okay, okay, be that way." Sean shook his head. "Won't return my calls, won't drink with me. You're a piece of work." He palmed Jack's shoulder.

"Don't touch me." Jack stared at the ground.

Sean spread his arms, the bottle in his left hand.

Jack grabbed it, stepped to the edge of the porch, and turned the bottle upside down.

"Hey, what are you doing?"

Jack emptied the last of the vodka and handed the bottle back. Sean held it up by its neck and tossed it on the lawn.

"Clean up your act," Jack said though his teeth.

"No need." Sean wiped his mouth with the back of his hand.

"You've got a business to run."

"Not anymore." Sean's eyes hardened.

"What are you talking about?"

"Logan & Sullivan is defunct, gone, kaput, extinct."

"Come again?"

"First we lost Richards, then Petersen, and then Donahue. You remember our three biggest clients?" Sean shrugged. "The rest soon followed. I had to liquidate all our positions. People were willing to take losses. They just wanted out."

"What did you do?"

"Not me, Jackie. You're not putting this on me. Oh no. I did my best. I gave it my all. But without you, they wouldn't stay."

Steve Richards, Chris Petersen, and Bill Donahue—clients whose money Jack had promised to look after. They left because of him. His company was gone because of him. He'd worked hard, given up so much for the business.

You lost Susan because of it.

"Your baby," Susan liked to say. "That business is your baby and sometimes I think you love it more than you love me."

Your baby. YOUR BABY. You destroyed your babies.

Jack froze. A choir ranted inside his head. *What have you done?* He covered his ears. He saw his clients shaking their heads. "We trusted you. We shouldn't have."

The voices grew louder. He saw his daughter's tiny coffin being lowered into the ground, dirt being tossed on it. "Daddy, please help me!"

The choir sang at a fevered pitch. "WHAT HAVE YOU DONE?"

"Stop!" Jack yelled. "Just stop!"

Sean looked at him as if he were an alien. He stepped back.

The ground was unsteady. Jack reached for the railing. He slipped, fell to his knees.

Sean's eyes and mouth were wide open. He stepped backwards, turned, and ran.

CHAPTER 28

DORIS CHANCE ANSWERED the door wearing jeans and a faded blue shirt with the top three buttons open—Jack could see freckles on her chest. She had long silver hair and lines around her eyes.

She has to be sixty.

"May I help you?" she asked.

"My name is Jack Logan. Alyson Walker is my wife's daughter. I was wondering if I could ask you some questions."

Doris Chance looked at his face. "You weren't married to Mary."

"No, Alyson was adopted," he said. "My wife was her biological mother." He was uncomfortable revealing this information to a stranger but knew he needed to give in order to get.

"Mary never said anything about that."

"I suspect she didn't, Mrs. Chance. I'm assuming she kept it from Alyson." He cocked an eyebrow. "May I come in?"

"I'd prefer you didn't. And as far as Alyson goes, we've told everything we know to the police."

"I know, but I was still hoping I could ask some follow-up questions. I've hired a private investigator. We're doing everything we can to find Alyson as quickly as possible."

"Why isn't the private investigator here?" She frowned. "Isn't that what you pay them to do?"

"He's following up on another lead. Like I said, we're trying to expedite the process."

"Like I said, we've already spoken to the police. Have your private investigator check with them. I'm sure they'll give you whatever information you need."

"We've already spoken to them, Mrs. Chance."

"Then you know I was the one who reported Alyson missing." Doris sighed. "She could be anywhere. She probably left the state. Mary had money." Doris glanced behind her. "You'll have to go. I've got a roast in the oven."

"Can I come back later?"

"I'm sorry, we're busy. Now if you'll excuse me, Mr. Logan, I need to get dinner ready for my family." She started to close the door. Jack put his hand on it.

"Mrs. Chance, please. I—"

"Where's your wife?" Doris craned her neck. "Is she out investigating another lead too?"

"She died." Jack swallowed hard. "In a car accident. Three months ago."

"My goodness." Doris covered her heart. "Losing a spouse is difficult."

"I'm trying to do what my wife would've wanted me to." Jack felt guilty using Susan's death this way. He pulled out his wallet, removed a photograph, and handed it to Doris. "This is her. Susan."

"The resemblance is amazing." Doris handed the picture back to Jack, shaking her head. "My deepest condolences."

"I saw Alyson yesterday." Jack's voice went higher.

"You found her?" Doris looked confused.

"She slipped away."

"Where did you see her?"

"At a place called the Rendezvous."

Doris opened the door all the way and said, "Come in." She held up her hand, spread her fingers. "But only for five minutes. You can't be here when Raymond gets home. My husband is very protective of his son." She looked up at Jack. "Do you understand?"

"Yes."

Inside, the smell of cooking meat filled the air. Jack's stomach grumbled. She led him to the den.

"I'll be right back," she said.

He sat on the couch. Two framed pictures were on the table behind it. He was about to look at them when Doris returned.

"This place…where you saw Alyson…" Doris eyed the chair next to her but remained standing.

"You mean the Rendezvous." Jack rose from the couch.

"It's a topless bar?"

Jack said, "Yes, but—"

"Alyson was working there?"

Jack nodded.

"What's she *thinking*?"

"She wasn't one of the dancers," Jack said.

"She's fifteen. What did she do there? Or should I be afraid to ask?"

"She was a cocktail waitress." Jack recalled the first time he saw Alyson. He shuddered and pushed the image away.

"She's a minor," Doris said. "That's illegal."

"Apparently she had fake ID."

"Alyson was resourceful when she needed to be, Mr. Logan. Very organized, very meticulous. You should've seen her room. Everything was in perfect order."

Jack swallowed a smile.

"Mary was a good mother," Doris continued. "She never

missed church and volunteered at the soup kitchen. She set a good example for her daughter. Why in the world would Alyson work there? It doesn't make a lick of sense."

"She was trying to get a part in a movie."

"What kind of movie?"

Jack recalled what Reggie said about John Walker: *He's into edgy stuff. There's violence and sex, but it's all subtle and very real.*

"I don't know much about it." Jack hoped they'd move off this topic.

"Well, I bet it's not rated PG!"

"Is there something you want to tell me, Mrs. Chance?" He suspected there was.

Doris studied him with her arms crossed. A ceiling fan above them mixed the air.

Come on, spill it. SPILL IT.

Doris reached into her pocket. "I found these when I was cleaning Nolan's room last week." She handed him a black pack of matches with the Rendezvous in gold script across the front. "Nolan is a good boy. Alyson was a good girl. I don't understand what's going on. I'm worried."

"Can I talk to Nolan?"

"Absolutely not! This situation has affected him."

"Mrs. Chance, he might know where she is."

Doris held up a hand. "I'll talk to him and let you know if I find out anything."

Jack opened the matchbook. 118 Holland was written in perfect block letters on the inside cover. It was the address Reggie had gotten from the Rendezvous.

He gave the matches back to Doris.

She opened the cover, nodded, and closed it.

"In case you're wondering, this isn't Nolan's handwriting."

"Were Alyson and Nolan close?" he said.

"Inseparable—since kindergarten. They were both shy,

good for one another." Doris pulled in a deep breath and let it out slowly. "Evidently Alyson has changed. It doesn't surprise me. I always sensed she was biding her time, waiting for an opportunity to prove something. I just never dreamed she'd do anything like this." Doris seemed to search his face. "Do you plan on being her legal guardian, Mr. Logan?"

Jack's body trembled.

The phone rang.

Thank you.

"Excuse me." Doris left the room.

Jack went over to the pictures behind the couch. He picked up one of Doris with a man and a boy—presumably Raymond and Nolan. The picture couldn't have been more than a year old.

Nolan was thin and muscular with big ears and a long face. He wasn't handsome. He was wearing a bathing suit and standing between his mother and father with a hand draped over each of their shoulders. He had red hair and was taller than his parents by a head. He didn't look like either one.

Maybe Nolan's adopted, too.

"Do I know you?" Jack heard someone ask. He spun around.

Nolan was standing behind him. He had on jeans, a white tee shirt, and a braided leather necklace.

"My name's Jack Logan."

Nolan's lips formed a circle.

"I'm looking for Alyson Walker," Jack said.

Nolan nodded, his mouth still open.

"Do you know where I can find her?"

"I...haven't seen her since..." Nolan looked hurt.

"When did you see her?" Jack moved closer.

Nolan pressed his lips together. His neck muscles bulged.

"Tell me!" Jack grabbed his shoulders and started shaking him. "Tell me, dammit. TELL ME." He shook harder. His mind was racing. Nolan's face contorted. "You've got to tell me.

You've got to!" Jack saw the fear in Nolan's eyes and stopped shaking him.

What the hell are you doing?

Nolan stomped down on Jack's foot.

"Damn." Jack dropped to a knee and grabbed his toe. "I'm sorry. I didn't mean to..."

"I saw her T...Tuesday." Nolan blushed. "Sorry."

Jack sucked in a breath. "No problem. Now we're even." He got up slowly.

"Nolan, what are you doing home so early?" Doris came into the room.

You're lucky she didn't see you shaking him.

"The coach...had an emergency. He had to leave early."

"Then please go upstairs and get ready for dinner." Her voice was gentle yet firm.

The boy looked at Jack and left the room. Doris picked up a recent photo of Nolan.

"This was taken at one of Nolan's swim meets. He's trying out for the Olympics. His coach thinks he could win a medal. He needs to stay focused. He lost Alyson, he can't lose this." She tightened her mouth. "My husband called. He's on his way home."

She saw Jack to the door.

"Can I call you tomorrow?" Jack was back on the front porch.

"I'll call you, Mr. Logan. You're in the phone book?"

Jack nodded. "Mrs. Chance, this is important."

"You have to understand. Things are complicated."

He couldn't argue with that.

CHAPTER 29

JACK WAS A BLOCK FROM HIS HOUSE when it occurred to him that Sean might be back when he got there. He ground his teeth. Of course he wouldn't. He was too drunk to drive and he had no idea how long Jack would be gone.

He parked his car in the driveway. It was seven-thirty. He hoped Reggie would call with some good news. He pictured Nolan Chance, standing in his living room with pain etched on his face. Nolan knew something.

You should've shaken it out of him.

He'd catch Nolan at school or a swim meet—someplace away from Doris.

He got out of the car, walked down the driveway, and got his mail. He flipped through it on the way up to his house.

He came to the telephone bill.

That'll have to wait.

Climbing the stairs to the front porch, he came to an envelope on the bottom of the pile. It had no return address.

At the top of the steps, he looked up. That's when he saw Alyson.

She was sitting on one of the rocking chairs. Her hands cupped her chin. She had on sneakers, torn faded jeans, and a tee shirt that said *Forever*.

Jack froze.

Alyson gave a start.

They held each other's gaze. Neither spoke.

She looked around as if she were weighing her options, including running away again. She probably didn't think he could help her, but he might be the best chance she had.

Maybe you're the only one she has.

"I'm sorry." Alyson stood up. "I'm sorry I ran away last night."

"I'm sorry I had to tell you everything I did, the way I did." He went up the last step and dropped the mail on the floor. "I had no choice."

"I know." Alyson shoved her hands in her back pockets. "Tara told me they're running background checks on everyone." She raised her eyebrows. "Can I come in?"

"Sure." Jack pulled out his keys and opened the front door, his heart hammering his chest.

Without heels Alyson was shorter than Susan, and in this light her hair wasn't as blond. But she had her mother's mouth and eyes.

She still looks just like Susan.

Alyson stepped past him. Her hair was damp. Maybe that's why it looked darker now. She stood in the hall, surveying her surroundings. Jack was behind her. She turned around and looked up at him. This was his wife's daughter, her flesh and blood. He shivered. Words escaped him.

"Could I have a glass of water?" she asked.

He nodded, grateful for this break in the tension. He headed toward the kitchen.

Alyson followed close behind.

He listened to her footsteps, his mind racing.

She stopped. He turned on his heels.

Alyson was looking up at the sun clock, her arms crossed.

"I like that."

"My wife bought it when we were in New Mexico." Jack spread his arms, noticed his fingertips trembling. "She bought everything here. Mementos from our vacations."

Alyson went over to the statue of The Thinker. She ran her fingers along its base, then jerked them away.

"We got that in Philadelphia. Susan said it reminded her of me."

Alyson shifted her gaze between Jack and The Thinker, her brow creased.

"I think she meant personality-wise." Jack almost smiled.

Alyson bent down and looked at the statue with her thumbs locked behind her back.

"Can you…"

"Can I what?" Jack stepped closer.

"Can you tell me some things about her?"

Images flooded his brain. There were so many things, how could he—

"Her favorite color was white," he said. "And she loved daisies—the white ones with yellow in the middle. She ran three times a week and meditated every morning." He closed his eyes. "She made me laugh when I thought I couldn't."

"How long were you… " Alyson looked down.

"Married?"

She nodded.

"It was two years." Jack felt dizzy. He held the table and steadied himself. "She was the only person I could talk to."

"I'm sorry, Mr. Logan." Alyson looked in pain.

"Sorry for what?"

"Sorry she died. And I could really use that glass of water now."

Jack nodded, then went into the kitchen and over to the sink.

Alyson sat down at the kitchen table. She folded her hands in front of her.

"Would you like something to eat?" He turned on the faucet and held his index finger under it until the water turned cold.

"Thanks, the water's fine for now."

Jack handed her a glass. She took it with both hands and drank half of the water.

He sat on the chair opposite her.

The air was cool. The refrigerator hummed, then came to an abrupt halt. Fading sunlight crept in from the picture window across from them. Children playing next door were howling.

He had an urge to speak.

Oh come on, Jackie boy—just tell her Susie's her mother and get this scene over with!

Alyson sipped some more water.

Jack's throat was parched. He swallowed. He was definitely getting a cold. He recalled last night, running in the rain, searching for the girl who had now found him.

Tell her before you get sick and die.

"I saw her accident." Alyson appeared to study the top of the table.

Jack stopped breathing.

Alyson swayed.

He was ready to catch her.

Who'll catch YOU?

She straightened up and looked straight into Jack's eyes. What she was saying didn't make sense, but he knew it was hard for her to say it, incredibly hard.

"I had something to do with how she died, Mr. Logan."

His head snapped back. She looked wretched.

"I don't understand," he said. "How can that be?"

She went over to the sliding glass doors that led out to the deck.

"I was about to go into the Rendezvous for my job interview when I saw a white Lexus coming towards me."

Jack watched her reflection in the glass.

"The passenger side window was open." Alyson looked at Jack from over her shoulder. "When she got closer, it was like seeing in a mirror. Your wife looked just like me."

Jack put his hand on Alyson's shoulder.

"We kept looking at each other." Her voice sounded choked. "There was no place for her to pull over. Then that cop car told her to keep moving."

Cop car?

He hadn't heard about that. Something they'd kept from him. Anger rumbled inside him. He suppressed it.

"Her car was going forward... while she was still looking back at me." Alyson turned toward Jack. "I was *screaming* and pointing to the truck her car was heading towards. But it was too late." She pulled a tissue from the pocket of her windbreaker and balled it in her hand.

Just like her mother used to do.

"Two men ran out of the electronics store. People were shouting." She took a breath. "I called 911 and waited on the corner until the police and ambulance came."

Jack sat back down at the kitchen table.

"I can't stop thinking about the way your wife looked at me. No one ever looked at me like that before."

"Susan had a phobia about driving in the city," he said. "She was on her way to the doctor. I was supposed to take her there. But I got stuck in traffic." He looked up. "It was my fault."

"No, it wasn't. She couldn't stop staring at me." Alyson met his eyes. "That's why she ran into the back of that truck."

CHAPTER 30

"Is THIS YOUR WIFE'S?" Alyson opened her hand. It was shaking. In her palm was a solid white-gold snowflake with an *A* inscribed on it. "I found this after everyone left. I had to keep it…. I mean, I…I just couldn't leave it there." She tipped her palm and the shiny snowflake fell into Jack's. Seated next to each other at the table, they both stared at it.

"I gave it to Susan." Jack studied the charm, its features sharp and clear in the white fluorescent light. He was being ripped apart from within. He would give the charm back to Alyson before she left, but for now he needed it near him.

He'd bought the snowflake after their first appointment with Dr. Gunn. He'd planned to buy her two more, one for each of their children. Three snowflakes for the three kids they wanted—each the same, each different. He would inscribe their child's first initial on each charm. It would be Alison, Brian or Brianna, and Christopher or Catherine—A, B, and C.

You had it all planned out.

"Snowflakes enchanted Susan," Jack said. "She refused to believe no two were alike." Jack recalled her sitting on their front steps on a winter morning, separating snowflakes in her palm, trying to find two that were identical.

"I can't believe that either," Alyson said. "I used to sit in my backyard and try to find two that were the same. My mother… she made fun of me for doing that."

"People make mistakes," he said to the top of her head, "even when they have the best intentions."

"I hope so," Alyson said softly. She looked up at him, her hair falling in front of her face. She pushed it away.

Jack dropped the charm into his shirt pocket, next to his heart. He patted it a couple of times and felt the sadness in Alyson's eyes.

"You sure you're not hungry?" he asked. "I could make you a sandwich."

He heard Alyson's stomach rumble. His did too.

"Do you have tuna fish?"

He sat up straight. "Do you like it with celery?"

"It's the only way to have it."

Susan wouldn't eat tuna unless it had celery.

Jack opened a can of solid white and drained the excess water into the sink.

"I can cut up the celery," she said.

"Great. It's in the bottom bin in the refrigerator." He pointed. "There's a knife in that drawer and a cutting board in the next one down."

Alyson gathered the items on the center island. Jack got a fork, a bowl, and a jar of mayonnaise and joined her. He looked over from mashing the tuna, admiring the neat, precise way she chopped the celery. He'd seen it before.

"Do you know why I was working at the Rendezvous?" Alyson asked.

"You want to be an actress."

"I have no interest in that." She used the knife to push the cut celery into the bowl. "My mother kept journals." Alyson started on the second stalk. "After she died, I read all of them."

"It's good you have them." Jack added a huge dollop of mayonnaise and tapped the spoon against the bowl.

"I knew most of what she wrote—my mother and I were close that way. She told me her problems. But one thing I didn't know was that my stepfather left her because we didn't fit into his life."

Jack stopped mixing. The Recluse Wife. Wasn't that what Roman called her? Alyson stopped chopping. Her body stiffened.

"I couldn't stop thinking about how that must've humiliated my mother." Her eyes hardened. "And me." She put down the knife, filled her glass with water, and took a sip. "Not long after that, I found out my stepfather was producing a movie and his stepson was the director." She resumed cutting, this time faster, harder.

Jack's eyes locked on her motions.

"I had this idea to get a part in that movie without my stepfather knowing." Alyson cut faster. "I tried to tell myself it was the worst idea in the *world*, but I kept imagining him coming to the set and seeing me there."

"You got the part." Jack put the mayonnaise back in the refrigerator. "You must've made quite an impression."

"I did some acting in high school. I never cared much for it, but I've been told I'm good." Her face darkened. She pointed the knife toward Jack. He flinched. "I did it to show that bastard how wrong he was about us."

Jack got out two plates and put two slices of whole wheat bread on each.

"So, why were you looking for me?" Alyson asked.

Jack froze.

"I… got that postcard that said you were missing. You look so much like Susan."

Alyson winced.

"It had been three months since her accident." Jack put the bread away. "I couldn't work anymore. I needed to do something…something worthwhile." He saw himself cleaning, submitting to the obsession that controlled him. "Finding you was it."

"Why?"

His heart pounded. His mind raced.

"Do you know why your wife couldn't stop looking at me?" Her voice broke.

The kitchen clock was ticking.

You need to figure this out quick.

"Please, Mr. Logan, tell me what you know."

He couldn't lie to her. He didn't want to hurt her.

You're trapped.

"Susan…" He took in a deep breath and held it.

There's a better way to tell her. FIND IT.

"What about her?" She moved closer.

"She was your mother."

Alyson buried her face in her hands.

The phone rang.

Neither of them moved.

It must be Reggie.

The answering machine picked up after the third ring.

Her hands fell away from her face.

She's not crying.

"You knew?" Jack asked.

"My father's name isn't on my birth certificate. My mother said it was artificial insemination. My mother had dark hair and brown eyes."

Alyson's are as clear blue as Susan's.

"My mother looked nothing like me and couldn't look me in the eye when she told me how I was conceived."

Her breathing became shallow, rapid. When she spoke, her voice was anguished.

"I lost her the moment I found her." She looked around, plucked the glass off the table and squeezed it so hard her fingertips whitened. "Now I'll never hold her."

"Alyson," Jack said. "You can't—"

"Why didn't Mary tell me about her? Why didn't she tell me about my mother?"

"She was probably—"

"I could've found her," she said, "I could've held her. She wouldn't be dead. Do you realize that? Your wife wouldn't be dead. My mother wouldn't be DEAD."

Alyson threw the glass.

It hit the far wall and shattered on the white marble floor. They both stared at the scattered pieces.

Jack's pulse raced.

"Why didn't she want me?" Alyson grabbed his arms. "Why didn't my mother want me?"

Jack couldn't speak.

"Did she ever talk about me?" A tear slipped down her cheek.

Jack stepped closer.

You can't lie to her.

Alyson hid her face in his chest.

He smelled her hair, his eyes closed. For a moment, it was Susan in his arms. Jack heard her saying, again, *You'll be a great father when the time comes.*

He looked down to face her daughter.

"I didn't find out about you until after she died, Alyson. But I do happen to know your mother loved you."

Tears lay on her cheeks. Pain twisted her face.

"She loved you from the day you were born until—"

Alyson's fists struck his chest. Her eyes blazed.

"How could you possibly know that? She DIDN'T EVEN TALK ABOUT ME!"

"I'll be right back."

CHAPTER 31

ALYSON SNIFFLED AS SHE unfolded the letter Jack handed her. She was still standing as she read it, her eyes questioning in some spots and softening in others. He couldn't see the page, but by her reactions Jack knew exactly where she was every word of the way.

She finished and her hands fell to her sides. She stared at the wall behind him. After a minute, she folded the letter and offered it back to him.

"You keep it. She wrote it to you." He gave her the envelope along with the copy of *Living Happy*. "Keep this, too. Your mother loved self-help books. This was her favorite."

Alyson put the letter in the book and held it against her chest. She started crying again, this time in silence, her body still.

He handed her a tissue.

"Thank you." Her fingers grazed his hand, her touch familiar. "You have pictures of her?" Alyson asked as she dabbed her eyes with the tissue.

"I've got plenty."

Susan had them in albums. Under each photo were the date, place, and a caption. Jack's two favorites were "Sitting on top of the world" from their hike to the top of Long's Peak in Colorado, and "Hanging down under," Susan hanging from a banyan tree in Australia.

He also had the pictures they collected for their wedding. Susan's father had photographed her standing in front of their house on each of her first sixteen birthdays, Susan always finding a way to strike a unique pose.

Then there was their wedding video. Jack had thought about this documentary of their wedding day along with the photos many times, but he could never look at them. He was about to show the video to Alyson when he remembered what else he had to tell her.

"You have an aunt, your mother's sister. Her name is Emily. She'd love to meet you."

Alyson smiled as she wiped away the last of her tears. At least she had a relative, a blood relative.

You can't let Emily adopt her.

"I'd like to meet her," Alyson said.

Jack's body trembled.

Now you've done it, Logan.

"But I had to," Jack said.

"You had to what?" Alyson asked.

"Nothing." Jack glanced at the white leather jacket on the chair next to Alyson.

"Is that my mother's?"

"Yes."

Susan always kept a jacket draped over the dinette chair. Jack put this one there after the accident. It had been there ever since.

Alyson ran her hand over the jacket. It was made of soft leather, had a ribbed waist, and zippers on the pockets and sleeves.

"Here, try it on." Jack held it open for her.

Susan's scent is still there.

Alyson held out her arms and slipped into it. The sleeves were perfect. The shoulders fell into place. She zipped it up, closed her eyes, and took in a deep breath.

"You can keep that." He was giving away something he thought he never would.

"No, I shouldn't." Alyson pulled down the zipper.

Jack held her arms. "It was made for you. Please keep it. I know she'd want you to."

"Thank you." She wrapped her arms around herself. "I love the way it feels."

"See, there's another reason to keep it."

Alyson suddenly grew serious. "Do you know anything about my father?"

Crap. Things were going so well.

"I mean, it's not you…is it?"

For a moment Jack imagined life with Susan and Alyson. He saw them riding bicycles, going to the beach, having a picnic, happy together.

"I…I'm not," Jack said. "But. . . "

You wish you were.

"But you know who is?"

He'd never wanted so desperately to lie.

"Yes."

"And he's alive?" Alyson raised her eyebrows.

He felt the hope moving through her.

"Yes." He could see Alan Dean sitting in his office, looking out the window, telling him and Emily he wanted nothing to do with his daughter, didn't want her attending Whitmore.

"And you know where he is?" Alyson asked.

"Yes."

"Is he married?"

"For twelve years."

"He has children?"

"No."

"And he knows about me."

"Yes."

Alyson looked at him, tears finding their way back into her eyes. She knew where this was going, but she still had to do it.

You can relate to that.

"He doesn't want to meet me." She looked at the wall where she'd thrown the glass. Jack stared at the broken pieces.

"I'm sorry, Alyson."

She pulled in a deep breath, then seemed to be looking at the broken glass fragments too.

"I still want to meet him." Her voice was firm.

Jack imagined Alyson in Alan Dean's office. The warm musty air, sounds from the college seeping in, Alan indifferent at best.

"Can you take me to him?" she asked.

He saw them driving up to Nestor in blinding sunlight, waves of heat rising off asphalt, his dread mounting by the mile. He began to sweat.

"He's not worth it, Alyson. Believe me."

"He's my father." Her anger returned. That part of her was unlike Susan. That part of her he hadn't expected.

"He's made it clear he doesn't want to get involved. He said it would be awkward."

"I'll handle it." She raised her chin. "You see your mother die, there's not much you can't handle."

She's probably right.

"What's his name?" Alyson asked.

"Alan Dean." Jack had a bitter taste in his mouth.

"Where is he?"

Jack looked down at the floor.

"Where is he?" Alyson stepped closer and caught hold of Jack's arms. "You can't keep this from me."

"He's a professor."

"Where does he teach?"

"Alyson, I'll help you any way I can, but you really need to give this some thought before—"

"I already have, and I need to meet him even if he rejects me. Please, Mr. Logan." She sounded desperate.

Well, he was desperate to protect her. But might *not* meeting Dean be worse for her than meeting him with no expectations? At least then she could close the book.

"He teaches at Whitmore College."

"Where is that?" she asked.

"In Nestor. Two hours from here."

"Will you take me?"

Now you've done it.

Jack's leg was shaking. His eyelid twitched. Alyson looked at him as if seeing him for the first time.

"I'm going with or without you. Nothing you can say will change my mind." She sighed. "You don't understand."

"I do understand."

Alyson appeared to study him. "So you'll take me?"

"No."

Alyson zipped up the leather jacket, picked up the book, and walked out into the living room and through the front door.

Let her go. Taking her to Dean would be too painful for you.

"I'm not afraid of pain."

You did the right thing. Move on.

"No, I need to protect her."

You can't. It's too late. Stop it here.

"So now that the story isn't going the way you planned, you can't continue?"

That's right.

"Don't be a fool. You can't end it here."

It's better that way. You don't see that?

"She shouldn't have to do this by herself."

This isn't about her. It's about you. It's always been about your redemption.

"Maybe it shouldn't have been. Maybe that was a mistake."

Jack felt what it would be like if Alyson didn't exist. If he were to never know what happened to her. He tried to picture his life an hour from now. He saw white.

"NO!" he cried as he ran out the front door.

Alyson looked up at him from the rocking chair.

"I'll take you," he said.

STOP.

Alyson smiled. "Thank you, Mr. Logan. Can we go tomorrow?"

He nodded.

"I have to leave now," she said. "I've got to meet a friend. He needs me."

Jack pictured Nolan in his room, watching the ceiling and thinking about her, wanting her more than Olympic gold.

"Come here at noon."

You can't let this happen. YOU CAN'T.

"I will. I'll see you then, I promise," she said. "Trust me."

"I do, Alyson."

"I can't believe you just let her go," Emily said.

"I had no choice."

They were on the phone. Jack was on the porch. The sun was going down.

"Nothing good can come of this," Emily said.

You know that.

"You're right."

"And yet you're still going to take her."

"Sometimes, Emily, the story doesn't end the way you want. Sometimes the characters just go in their own direction."

WEDNESDAY, APRIL 2, 2008
WESTCHESTER, NEW YORK

HE PUSHED THE CHAIR AWAY from his desk and rubbed the back of his neck. The clock on his computer said he'd been working for two hours. It felt like minutes.

He stretched his arms above his head and eyed the screen. The cursor blinked at the end of the last sentence. He closed his eyes and imagined the next scene. Thought about how he could show, not tell, the frustration and anger he wanted to convey. He snapped his fingers and rolled his chair back to the keyboard. Typed one sentence. Read it. Scowled and deleted it. He took a breath, typed another sentence. After reading it, he deleted that one too.

Write shitty first drafts, that's what he'd read. But it wasn't that way with him. He had to get each sentence perfect before he could go on to the next. It cost him weeks of frustration before he realized that.

There was a knock on the door. He clenched his jaw. He hated being disturbed, especially when he was writing. But he'd hide his frustration. He was good at deception.

"Good morning, sir," the young man said.

"Hello, Roman."

Roman came five days a week, always around the same time, always with the same happy voice. The girl came on weekends. She was shy and barely spoke. He preferred the girl.

Roman handed him a pill and a cup of water. He was sure Roman was checking out the room, probably in his job description.

"You've been writing."

"You can tell?"

Roman smiled. "You have that look."

"What look?" He tensed. He told himself to relax. In the presence of others he had to remain calm.

"Peaceful," Roman said. "You look very peaceful."

He *did* feel at peace when he was writing, but it bothered him that Roman sensed it. He hid his feelings, though they prodded him to get in touch with them.

"And what do I look like when I'm not writing?"

"Actually, you've been pretty calm lately." Roman shoved a hand into his pocket. "Much better than…well, you know…"

"I do?" He enjoyed making this intruder uncomfortable.

"I'm sorry, Mr. Logan. I didn't mean to imply that—"

"That's okay." He handed the cups back to Roman. "No offense taken."

Roman wished him a good day and closed the door behind him.

He looked out the window. The benches on the lawn were empty. Carlos was mowing. The sky was slate gray. The forecast called for rain, but he didn't mind. The sun depressed him.

He sat at the computer and typed a line. He read it, didn't find a flaw. Read it again. Still no reason to change it. He typed the next sentence. Then another. Words flowed onto the page. He stopped and reread the first sentence. He looked for words to eliminate. He found three. There was more he could do with it. He'd revise it until he couldn't any more.

There was another knock on the door. He picked up a pencil and broke it in two.

"I'm sorry to bother you," a young woman said. "We need to reschedule your appointment with Dr. Murphy."

"What? Why?" Frustration howled inside him.

"There's a conflict…it was my mistake." She looked toward the floor. "He needs to see you in an hour."

"It's no problem."

If you'll just control your damn emotions.

Everything was a test. No room for failure. He had to get out of here.

"Hello, Rebecca," Jack said as he stood in front of an open window.

"Hello, Mr. Logan." She smiled as she looked up from whatever she was doing. She used a pen to point to her right. "Have a seat. He'll be with you shortly."

Jack sat furthest from the door. He took a deep breath, closed his eyes, and let his imagination roam.

He and Alyson enter Alan Dean's office. Dean looks up at Alyson, surprised, hostility stamped across his features. "I don't want to see you." He points at Jack. "Didn't he tell you that?" Jack can't speak. Alyson says, "He told me. I made him take me anyway." She steps closer. Dean moves away. "I want nothing to do with you." Alyson glares at him. "You owe me this." Dean points to the door. "I don't owe you a damn thing. Now both of you leave." Jack reaches into his pocket and pulls out a gun. He holds it with both hands and points it at Dean. "You son of a bitch. Hear what she has to say or I'll blow your head off."

***

Dr. Murphy closed the black three-ring binder. The yellow legal pad on his desk had two pages of notes he'd compiled.

He tightened his tie and adjusted his silver stickpin. He pressed the button on his intercom.

"Rebecca, please send Mr. Logan in."

A moment later, the door opened and a thin man with black curly hair stepped into the room. He was wearing dark slacks and a white button-down shirt open at the collar.

Dr. Reginald Murphy had been treating Jack Logan for nearly a year now—three sessions a week in which Jack would lie down and free associate for an hour.

Jack headed toward the couch.

"Please, over here." Dr. Murphy pointed to one of the club chairs in front of his desk. Jack hadn't sat there since their first session.

He took a seat.

"I finished reading your manuscript." Murphy held up the thick black binder.

They stared at one another.

Silence.

"Don't you want to know what I think of it?" the doctor asked.

Jack pointed to himself. "You mean I finally get to ask a question?"

Dr. Murphy smiled and leaned back in his thick leather chair. "Is there more to the story?" The doctor examined his fingernails.

"It ends there." Jack gripped the arms of his chair.

"I see the merit in that."

"I thought you'd want me to finish it."

"I want you to do what you want to do. That's a fundamental aspect of your treatment." Murphy opened the middle drawer and pulled out a nail file. "If you write more of this story, I'd like to read it.

"You're the only one who will."

Murphy put a check next to his last note. "But you'll work on another book?"

"It's like what Gloria Steinem said: 'Writing is the only thing that, when I do it, I don't feel I should be doing something else.'"

Murphy made a note. "And what about Emily, have you spoken to her?" he asked.

"Only once since the accident."

"How does that make you feel?"

"Sad."

"Why?"

"I want her to forgive me. I need someone in Susan's family to, but I don't think that's ever going to happen."

"Would you be willing to reach out to them?" Something Murphy wouldn't have suggested before.

"I've tried. There's been no response."

"Have you given any more thought as to why you wrote this book?"

"Like I said. It came to me, one chapter at a time." Jack crossed his legs.

Dr. Reginald Murphy had treated many patients with extreme anxiety during his twenty-five years as a clinical psychologist, but none of them had ever written a fictional account of their neurosis while he treated them.

"How do you feel about leaving West Wind?" Murphy looked out the window behind him. Jack had been admitted to West Wind following a nervous breakdown a week after his wife's accident. He'd been there ever since.

"I'm looking forward to it." Jack followed the doctor's gaze.

"Good." Dr. Murphy stood and sat on the edge of his desk, one leg dangling. "I'll see you once a week as an outpatient." He shrugged. "But call me any time you need me. That doesn't change."

"I appreciate that, doctor. I appreciate all you've done."

Dr. Murphy wanted to shake Jack's hand, but he'd stick to

his rule of no physical contact during treatment. He checked his watch.

"Let's end here for today. There's more to be done, but you've worked hard. You deserve a break."

"Thank you." Jack slipped his hands into his pockets. And smiled.

It was the first time Murphy had seen his patient do that.

Ten minutes later, Jack was back in his room.

It was sparse and neat, the walls painted white. The wood floors shone. A sun clock hung on one wall over a table with a statue of The Thinker and a marble chess set. He'd pack them in the morning.

Jack was seated at the oak desk. The top of it was clear, except for a banker's lamp in the corner. It had been a year since the day that cut his life in two—everything that happened before the accident, everything that happened after.

He opened the desk's side drawer and removed a file labeled Someday/Maybe.

It was two p.m. West Wind was quiet. Most of the staff was at lunch.

He opened the file, his hands trembling.

"Where is it?" He asked the question softly but out loud. The door to his room was closed.

He pushed aside an ad for hot yoga classes, threw an article on aromatherapy to the floor. He grabbed a business card for a palmist and tore it to pieces.

His heart palpitated. It had to be there. IT HAD TO BE THERE. His breathing quickened.

He rifled through the rest of the papers in the folder.

It wasn't there.

HOW CAN THAT BE?

It should've been right on top.
He had to find it.
He had to find the postcard.
He had to find that missing girl.

EPILOGUE

DR. MURPHY TURNED AWAY from the monitor. Earlier he had watched the recording of his patient's actions from the very first episode at West Wind. Not that he needed to view it to recall every detail.

Dr. Murphy had been treating Jack Logan for three years now.

"He always searches for the postcard the day before he's scheduled to leave?" Emily, the real Emily, sat across from Dr. Murphy. She wore a blue business suit. She looked just like the woman Jack described in *Have You Seen Her?*, though more reserved and a little anxious.

"Yes." Dr. Murphy imagined his med school mentor, a man who drilled him in patient confidentiality, rolling over in his grave as the doctor revealed patient information to someone he hardly knew. Or did he know her, through Jack Logan's book? What was true and what was Jack's imagination? Murphy was having a hard time remembering.

Jack wrote *Have You Seen Her?* after his initial breakdown during his first year of treatment. At the time, Jack appeared to be functioning better with each session. His grief would always be there, but Murphy believed Jack was starting to become aware of his weaknesses, the first step in controlling them.

Then the second breakdown came.

Roman had found Jack in his room frantically going through his desk drawers, trying to find a postcard. The patient was distraught, believing that it was in one of his file folders.

They calmed Jack, eventually, but it was a setback. The therapy started again. A year later, Dr. Murphy was hopeful, thinking that his time Jack Logan was ready to leave West Wind, that this time it was for real. It wasn't.

By the third time, Murphy was fearful. The pattern was always the same. Dr. Murphy met with Jack the day before his discharge. All would go relatively well until Jack went back into his room and looked for a non-existent postcard with a picture of a missing girl.

Murphy decided at that point that he would wait for Jack to rebound and then try a different approach. He might have to compromise his principles, but he was running out of options. And this, he reminded himself, was an unusual situation.

The police had provided Dr. Murphy with a copy of their accident report on the death of Susan Logan. *Have You Seen Her?* hadn't been that far from reality. The crash had occurred near a gentleman's club named the Rendezvous, and there was an electronics store on the corner. The truck Susan ran into was doubled-parked in a loading zone just as Jack depicted. Susan had been looking back according to one witness, but there was no explanation as to why. There was no Alyson or anyone like her. The accident was called in by patrolman John McKenna.

Curious, Murphy went to the Rendezvous one Sunday evening. It wasn't as Jack had described. Not at all. There was no long hallway with pictures of models. There were two small bars as opposed to the one big one, and no raised stage. There were no booths where men could sit with exotic dancers. Dr. Murphy concluded Jack had never been there.

Then a waitress in a tight white dress walked up to him. She had dark hair and deep, blue eyes, but her eyebrows were blond. When she said her name was Candace, Murphy dashed out of there like Jack did at the beginning of chapter twenty-five. Driving home, Dr. Murphy knew what he had to do—and it wasn't to find Alyson Walker.

Emily White lived alone. Dr. Murphy found her through a friend of a friend, who agreed to send her an email. Emily responded, and she and Dr. Murphy exchanged a dozen messages. Then he visited her on a spring afternoon. Her house was just as Jack had described: a castle with a red sedan parked in a circular driveway. Emily was standing by the front door. Probably in the same spot where Jack had written he left her off after she confessed to having had Alyson's postcard sent to him.

It was the first time Dr. Murphy had met Susan Logan's half-sister and he was doing so with the understanding that there was something he thought she should read. Immediately upon meeting her, the doctor couldn't help but feel there could be more to this than he originally thought.

Emily smiled and shook his hand. She had a firm yet gentle grip. She invited him inside for something to drink. He politely declined, gave her a copy of *Have You Seen Her?*, and left.

Dr. Murphy was committed to this course and needed to let things play out with as little interference from him as possible. For everyone's sake.

Emily sent him a long email that night. The guilt over not contacting Jack had been eating at her she said. It was the first time she admitted it. Emily agreed to meet Dr. Murphy at his office the next day. There now seemed to be a sense of urgency on her part.

"Jack wrote this?" she asked after she was seated in front of Dr. Murphy's desk.

"Every word of it." Murphy took a nail file out of the center drawer and began filing, a habit he purposely formed.

His mentor had taught him to have an outward habit so that patients who needed to could focus on that and not on looking for other distractions.

"I am just like that." Emily's hand was shaking as she put *Have You Seen Her?* on top of his desk. "He got me pretty much right."

Dr. Murphy sat back in his chair and reminded himself that this was not a patient.

"He's a writer now?" Emily had bright green eyes. "He used to trade stocks."

"It's something he always wanted to do."

"He never told us about that."

"He finished *Have You Seen Her?* a year after the accident. He hasn't written anything since." Murphy continued filing.

"Is this about writer's block?" Susan Logan's sister appeared confused. Distraught, even. "Do you want me to help with that?"

"No." Dr. Murphy sat up. "Ms. White, I want you to help Jack Logan leave West Wind."

"Me?" she pointed to herself.

"Yes." He wondered if she knew what he was asking of her. "Jack has unresolved issues with the others he's written about, but it's you he wants and needs forgiveness from. Ms. White—"

"Emily." She almost smiled. "You know more about me than most people. You can call me Emily."

"I think you can save him. Will you try?"

Emily paused. She hesitated so long he thought she would refuse. But no. "Yes, doctor. It's about time I do." She appeared to relax.

It was then that Dr. Murphy smiled and envisioned Jack Logan beginning the next chapter in his life.

Pray for the missing children
and their families.

10% of the profits from *Have You Seen Her?*
will be donated to organizations focused
on finding missing children.

Coming Soon: *Remember*
By Rich Silvers

Confronted by his lover's infidelity, Julian Barnes perpetrates a reckless act. Unexpectedly, his actions seem to make his life all he ever wanted it to be. The only problem? Julian doesn't remember what he did, and now he's obsessed with discovering the truth.

Chapter 1

Julian made bets with fate.

Like his tank would fill before the next car pulled into the gas station. He'd reach the cashier before the person in the other line. The 1812 Overture ends before his exit. He'd wager something he wanted to be true.

Julian kept his foot off the brake as he headed towards the intersection. The light was red. He wasn't going to stop. He had tried this once before but didn't go through with it.

Now he would.

He had just found Julia in bed with someone else, and if he could make it through the intersection without crashing then he wouldn't lose her.

His car moved at thirty miles an hour on a two lane road that cut through the heart of Nestor—a small upstate town near Sunrise Hospital. McCann's bar was on one corner, a bank on the other. It was nine p.m. on a Friday in October.

Julian was going down a steep hill. His mind was blank. The pain was gone. He wasn't concerned about damaging his vehicle, a rise in insurance rates, or a moving violation. Nor injury. Not even death. He just kept going.

Julian's speedometer was up to thirty-five, his body relaxed.

An SUV passed through the intersection.

Julian's foot moved toward the brake. It froze.

He hadn't even seen the man's face. He'd only seen Julia's back and her long thick black hair as she looked up, pelvis writhing, screaming obscenities.

He loved Julia's back—a luscious curve that ended at heart-shaped buttocks. He inhaled and smelled her. He licked his lips and tasted her.

He was forty yards away.

Julia loved to be touched. He loved to touch her. She'd lie on the bed and he'd trace his fingers down her spine. Time fell away. She'd moan, "Don't stop." He couldn't.

Thirty yards away.

A half hour earlier Julian stood in the doorway of Julia's bedroom, expecting her to notice him any moment. But she was too focused on what she was doing.

Twenty yards.

He should've cleared his throat, stomped his foot, or tapped her shoulder. But he had to leave. He couldn't take the stench of sex. Not any longer.

Ten yards away.

The light was still red.

His speedometer read fifty.

**Find out more about this book at
www.RichSilvers.com**